TALK TO THE HAND

KARI LEE TOWNSEND

OLIVER-HEBER BOOKS

TALK TO THE HAND

KARI LEE TOWNSEND

1

ZAPPED!

"Oh, my God, you're not going to believe this!" I spoke in my cell phone to my best friend, Melody Stuart, as I cut through the woods from her house to mine. Thank you fashion gods for the layered look. Shivering, I buttoned my short blue velour jacket over my long black and silver sparkly tanks to keep out the September evening air.

We lived in the Adirondack Mountains, and the sun had made it hard to see. I'd been a Girl Scout since forever. This should not be happening to me! "I'm lost," I said.

"Again?" Melody the Drama Diva shrieked right on cue.

I'd moved to Blue Lake from the west coast at the beginning of summer, and was nervous about meeting new friends. But when I showed up to soccer camp the first day and saw that Melody wore the same vintage ribbon around her pony-tailed hair, I knew I'd met my partner in crime.

"Samantha ... how do you get lost? You, Ms. Queen of Technology, who gets the latest everything. Doesn't your new cell phone have that built in find-my-way-anywhere thingy?"

"Yeah, but my mom works for Electro. She practically gets all that stuff for free."

"You're lucky."

Mel wished she had parents like mine: ones who bought her whatever she wanted. Hers never gave her anything except their time.

"No, <u>you're</u> lucky," I said. "I'd love to have a brother or sister."

Mel was the oldest of five children, with a stay at home mom and a teacher for a dad. They might not have a lot of money, but they did a ton of family stuff. I'd trade all my electronics to have my parents back together.

"Quit changing the subject. How did you get lost again?"

I groaned. "I know I have this awesome phone, and everything. But the extra navigation thing doesn't do me much good when I'm too busy texting and talking to you to remember to turn it on. It's got all these crazy functions and apps. I still haven't figured out how to use half of it."

"I'm surprised your mom gave you something so high tech. It's not like any cell phone I've ever seen."

"I was surprised, too, but whatever. It's mine now." I hit the speaker phone icon and stepped over a fallen tree trunk, trying not to snag the green satin ribbon on my black leather ballet flats as I sat down to program the GPS feature for home. "My getting lost is your fault, too, you know."

"Nice try, genius." Melody's voice rang out even louder through the speaker, making her tone anything but melodious.

"I try," I said, grinning.

"Well, try harder. This one is all you, there, Dorothy." She snorted. "You'd better click your heels and follow the yellow brick road home before your mom sounds the alarm. I've seen how she gets when you miss curfew."

"You have no idea." My mom is the queen of sophistication. A top executive with a calm but aggressive manner. She never loses her cool about anything, except when it comes to my safety. She wouldn't stop short of turning this town upside down to find me. "See you in school tomorrow."

I hung up, still holding my fully-charged, top-of-the-line little friend as though it was Dorothy's ruby red slippers and my ticket home. My phone was my life. What if someone special wanted to text me? I was officially a teenager now. My eighth grade year. New home. New school. New friends. I just wanted to be accepted, to fit in. And, okay, to experience my first kiss. I'd even picked out the perfect boy.

Trevor Hamilton.

I sighed dreamily as I stood and wiped off the back of my low-rise jeans, then held the GPS feature of my phone up before my eyes. Squinting, I struggled to see the map since I didn't have my glasses on, and I'd turned the volume down. That annoying, monotone talk-like-I-have-an-IQ-of-ten voice drove me nuts. I'd rather take my chances following the highlighted route, even if I did wind up in Oz.

The colorful fall leaves, twigs and acorns crunched beneath my feet and the smell of pine hung heavy in the air, reminding me of the cleaner Gram used. I picked up the pace, knowing my mom would call out the cavalry if I was more than five minutes late. The last thing I wanted was for Trevor's dad, Sheriff Hamilton, to come to my rescue--again!

A light up ahead caught my attention, and I prayed to the god of have-pity-on-me it wasn't a search party with a flashlight. As I walked closer, I wilted. No Sheriff Hamilton in sight, just ... well, I wasn't sure.

It wasn't like anything I'd ever seen.

I came to a stop and stared at an enormous hole in the ground with a bright blue-green light shining within. I needed to get home, but curiosity grabbed hold of me and wouldn't let go. Like discovering where your parents hid your Christmas gifts and trying to resist the urge to take a peek.

I crept forward, trembling a little. Maybe it was a new kind of rare gem, and I would be the first one to discover it. I'd be famous. Now that would definitely make the other students at Blue Lake Junior High think I was cool.

I hurried my steps until I stood on the edge of the hole, then blinked rapidly. What the heck was it? It was huge and sort of looked like a crystal, except it glowed so bright it hurt my eyes. It smelled like the time my mom forgot she had eggs boiling.

I was no science dork, but it didn't take a genius to figure out this thing wasn't "of this world." A need to know what it felt like settled over me. It looked sort of watery, yet solid. Just one little touch. What could it hurt? I touched the tip of my finger to the freaky glowing crystal-type thingy.

Not a good idea.

A force more powerful than anything I'd ever experienced ripped through my body, feeling like I was having surgery with no anesthesia. The glowing blue-green light illuminated my insides until I screamed in agony, the smell of burning flesh turning my stomach seconds before the force threw me twenty feet backwards.

I landed hard, the breath whooshing out of my lungs, my eyes rolling back, knocked out cold like I'd gone a round with Oscar Delahoya. Moments later, I opened my eyes, pain free and smelling like me again: cucumber melon body splash and mint double-stuffed Oreo cookies.

I fixed my standard ponytail and examined my body, but couldn't find a single burn mark, cut, bump or bruise. I felt strong and energized. The only thing I found was the tiny chocolate stain from eating cookies at Melody's house on my new coat, and a ton of dirt and grass stains on my new jeans.

"What the heck happened?" I said out loud to hear my voice and make sure I wasn't dead. I couldn't wait to tell Melody. I had to send her a picture. I glanced around.

My elation over having survived my "close encounter" evaporated as fear filled my every pore. The kind of fear only royally ticked off parents can instill. Scrambling to my feet, I searched the ground for a good ten minutes. I looked everywhere: under rocks, trees, leaves, you name it. I even retraced my steps, but found nothing. Forget the stains on my new clothes, I couldn't find my Electro Wave anywhere. I might not be dead now, but I would be when I got home.

My parents were going to kill me.

"YOU'RE LUCKY I DIDN'T CALL SHERIFF HAMILTON, YOUNG lady. I was just about to. Do you know how worried I was?" my mother, Victoria O'Reily-Granger, swept her precisely cut, styled, and highlighted blond bob behind her ears, then crossed her arms over her cream silk blouse, her blue eyes sizzling. She stood as tall as her impressive five-foot-ten inch frame would allow, tapping her imported slipper on the hard wood floor.

I took after my dad--medium brown hair, medium brown eyes, and medium height. Trevor looked more like my mom--beautiful. That could be a problem, if my parents were any example.

Fairy tales could only last so long, and Beauty and the Beast were never meant to be. Okay, so my dad wasn't a beast, but he sure as heck wasn't Prince Charming all the time. Then again, my mom had her Wicked Witch of the West moments. Maybe they really were better off apart. That thought turned my stomach, and then I bit my bottom lip as another disturbing thought hit me.

Did that mean Trevor and I were better off just friends?

"You should have called to tell me you were going to be late," my mom finally said, pulling me away from my depressing thoughts.

"I know. I'm sorry. I thought you were going to be mad because I got lost again." Stained clothes safely hidden in my room, I plopped my sweat suit clad butt on the Italian leather sofa in our great room, and tucked my freezing feet beneath the afghan Gram had made.

FYI: the only comfortable, homey thing in the entire room. I sighed. Where was Gram when I needed her? She seemed to be the only one who got me. Sometimes I wished I still lived with her.

"I'm not mad, I was just worried. Anything could have happened to you out there." My mom walked across the Persian throw rug, stopping to straighten a crystal figurine perched slightly off center in the middle of the glass coffee table. Sometimes I felt like I lived in a museum instead of a home. Guess Dad had felt the same since he was the messiest person I knew.

"Mom, nothing happened," I said, recapturing her attention. "See, I'm fine." I spread my arms wide. No way would I tell her about the "incident." She'd haul my butt off to the nearest emergency room and keep me out of school for a week. I wasn't about to miss a chance to talk to Trevor again.

I'd started crushing on him the second I first saw him at football camp over the summer. Mel liked a boy named Scott Randolph, so she'd dragged me with her and introduced me to everyone. Trevor talked to me, but there was something about him. Like he wouldn't let anyone get too close. His mom died a few years back, so maybe that had something to do with it. It made me want to get through to him even more.

Now that school had started, fate had intervened, giving me the chance. Trevor's locker was right next to mine. We also shared a homeroom. Missing school was not an option. Not to mention, tomorrow night was my first soccer game.

"Cell service goes in and out by the minute, depending on where you're standing, especially in the woods." My mom's voice cut through my thoughts. "What if the battery on your phone had died?" Her voice softened, and she sat beside me. "I just want you to be more careful, honey. That's all."

"I know, and I will. I promise."

"Okay." She gave me a quick hug, her exotic perfume teasing my nose, reminding me of our house in San Jose-- the Silicon Valley part of northern California. The three of us had lived there together as a family before everything fell apart.

"You're still in trouble, young lady. Fork over your Electro Craze." Holding out her hand, she wiggled her long, elegant manicured fingers.

"When did they change the name to Electro Craze?" I asked. "The box you gave me said Electro Wave."

She frowned, wrinkling her forehead. "I've never heard the name Electro Wave. You must have read the box wrong." She swiped her hand through the air. "Doesn't matter. Your privileges will be taken away for a couple of weeks."

It suddenly hit me what she'd asked for. "You want my cell like now?" She nodded, and I swallowed hard. How could I have forgotten? I decided to just tell her. Maybe my honesty would help my case. "Um, well, about that." I widened my eyes, hoping to look innocent, vulnerable, help-less. Anything to kick her motherly instincts up a notch, and make her go easy on me. "I kind of, sort of ... lost it in the woods."

"What did you just say?" my mother said in a calm but stern tone with a hard look in her eyes that would bring top executives to their knees. "Do you know how much that cell phone cost?"

"Don't you get like a huge discount since you got that promotion?" I squeaked.

My mother just stared at me. Finally, she clenched her jaw and pursed her lips, going into full blown Evil Queen Mode. "That is beside the point. I think we've been way too lenient with you, Samantha Marie Granger. You're a teenager now and obviously spoiled. It's time you took responsibility. No more gadgets until you can prove you can handle them. And don't think you can go to your father to play us against each other. He'll agree with me on this one," she said, then muttered more to herself, but I heard her anyway, "or so help me God; he'll pay even more."

So much for honesty helping my case. I never asked for anything other than a piece of them, but they gave me a piece of the material world instead. A piece by the name of Electro Wave--I know what I saw. Now they wanted to take it all away. Talk about harsh.

"You can't be serious. How am I supposed to listen to music, or talk on the phone, or, or ... not get lost," I sput-tered, desperate enough to say anything.

"Might I remind you that you got lost with a built-in GPS?" Her perfectly shaped blond brow crept up, and the corners of her lips tipped down. "In fact, how did you get home if you lost your navigation system?"

"I ... I don't know," I said, just now realizing I didn't have to think twice earlier. Even in the dark, I had known exactly where I was going, but I hadn't questioned it at the time. I'd kind of had more important things on my mind. Like trying to find a way to tell my mom I'd lost my cell phone without her killing me.

Maybe a better sense of direction was a side effect of the incident, and I would no longer need the GPS feature. Still, that didn't solve my communication problem. How would I live without texting? I wanted, no, I <u>needed</u> my phone.

"Please, Mom," I begged. "I'll do anything."

"Sorry, sweetie, it's not going to work. It's time you grew up. There are consequences for your actions in life. You need to start learning that now."

Anger surged through me at the injustice of it all. This wasn't fair. It wasn't even my fault. "My phone is my life, Mom. You can't do this to me."

"I can, and I did." Her ice-blue eyes locked onto mine and narrowed into her Angelina Jolie impersonation: I-brought-you-into-this-world-I-can-take-you-out stare. No way would I win this argument. "Guess you'll have to find some other means to entertain yourself. From this day forward, your life is about to change in a big way."

2

CAN YOU HEAR ME NOW?

The next morning at breakfast, missing my Electro Wave desperately--I refused to call it anything else--I poured the milk into my Wheeties: the breakfast of champions. I would do anything to improve my skills for tonight's soccer game.

I yawned, then took a sip of orange juice. I'd hardly slept at all last night, too wired after all that had happened. The last big change to happen to me had been when my parents announced they were getting a divorce almost one year ago.

They both worked for Electro, a huge electronics corporation. After having some big fight over who knows what, they separated. Sometimes I wondered if they were splitting up because of me, but they always said I had nothing to do with it. I went to live with Gram in Los Angeles until Mom transferred to Blue Lake, but I still hadn't come to terms with any of it.

The thought of them divorcing was worse than starting my period for the first time ever on the first day of school in sixth grade. I'd leaked all over my new white cotton pants. To this day, I refused to wear white again. But I wasn't stupid. No way would I give up my Seven's. They were the best jeans on earth. Having my phone taken brought me right back to that first day of sixth grade.

Gut wrenching.

Extreme boredom and isolation settled over me. There was <u>nothing</u> to do. I sat there, pushing the whole wheat flakes around in the milk.

My mom breezed into the kitchen in her burgundy pin-striped suit looking like the poster child for successful female businesswomen. "Don't forget to take your vitamin." She slid her briefcase on the granite counter top on the island in the kitchen, and fixed herself a bran muffin to go with her coffee as she read the paper. "Oh, my. Did you see this?"

"See what?" I set my dishes in the sink and peeked over her shoulder to scan the article she pointed at, then choked on my vitamin.

"Careful." She patted me on the back, handing me my glass of juice as she returned her gaze to the paper. "It says here two hikers came upon some bizarre discovery in the woods early this morning. 'An unidentified foreign object.' They didn't go near it for fear it was radioactive since it was glowing." She looked up from her paper with concern. "You didn't see anything like that, did you?"

"No," I lied. It was bad enough she took away my gadgets. I shuddered to think what she'd do if she knew I touched that weird thing.

What if it really was radioactive?

I swallowed hard, my breakfast creeping up my esopha-gus. Feeling queasy, an image of my insides glowing and the smell of burning flesh flashed before my eyes. My flesh. I shivered. What if I grew a third boob or something? That would be just my luck, not to mention pretty much kill any shot I had with Trevor.

"Promise me you'll stay out of that area of the woods until the Powers That Be deem it safe. Lord only knows what kind of contaminates it left behind." I nodded, and she looked back at the article. "I guess they've already moved the object to a lab for special team of scientists to examine it. Well, that should put Blue Lake on the map. Not much exciting happens in this small town, does it?"

"G-Guess not," I managed, my throat still sore from choking. Third boob here I come. I'd have to Google radioactivity and see if I could find some special solution to cleanse my system.

I watched my mom stir a fine powder in her orange juice, drink it down, and swallow her own vitamins. Reading the label, I thought, now there's an idea. Mom's Metamucil.

"Whoops. Excuse me," Mom said, dabbing the corners of her mouth with a napkin.

Then again, maybe not. Having gas wasn't any more attractive than growing a third boob.

"You sure you're up to playing soccer tonight? You don't look so good." She felt my forehead.

"I'm okay. Just tired. I'll take a power nap on the bus ride to the game, I promise."

"Who do you play again?"

"White Peak, why?"

"Well, I don't have a meeting this afternoon, so I thought I'd get done early and come to your game. Where is White Peak, anyway? Never mind, I'll use Map Quest to find it. You're not exactly good with directions." She winked.

A massive pain sliced through my brain, and my vision blurred. I winced, feeling as though gears shifted beneath my skull like I had a machine inside my mind. Suddenly, my head tipped forward, then left, and my nose twitched six times in rapid concession. With a will of their own, my lips puckered five times.

I turned to my mother and said, "Drive five miles northwest, turn left at the Wal-Mart, go one mile more, turn right at the Home Depot. The school is fifty yards at the end of the road on the right. Estimated distance: six point two miles. Estimated time: seven minutes."

Mom's coffee cup halted half way to her lips as she gaped at me. I couldn't blame her since I'd shocked myself. The words had come out of my mouth in my voice, but the tone and speed at which I'd talked had been one hundred percent GPS.

"Coach gave us directions," I said in my normal voice, then added, "Hey, look at the time. You're going to be late for work, and I'm going to be late for school. See you at the game." I dashed upstairs to my bedroom and slammed the door, my heart racing faster than a megabyte. My head still ached, and my vision was still slightly blurry.

Ohmigod, what the heck was that all about?

I paced back and forth, blinking and wringing my hands on the verge of hysteria. What was happening to me? First, I knew how to get home last night, and now I know the exact directions to the last mile for how to get to my game. Something was wrong. I stopped pacing. Stress. It had to be stress. Either that or I was going crazy. My cell phone started to ring, and I jumped. Wait a minute...

My lost cell phone.

I searched every inch of my room, but couldn't find my Electro Wave anywhere. That confirmed it. Look out nuthouse here I come. I tried to keep panic from taking over. What was I going to do? I scratched my palm which itched something fierce. With my luck, the third boob would sprout out of my palm. I glanced down and let out a little yelp.

No boob, but ... good God, my hand was ringing.

I held it up in front of my face and felt my eyes bulge in horror. My palm glowed the same shade of bright blue-green as the crystal in the woods. My skin became transparent with the veins forming a screen the size of a cell phone, and little brail-type bumps in the shape of numbers pushed up beneath the surface.

"Ewww!" I shook my hand, frantically trying to make it go away, but it wouldn't stop. "This can't be happening to me," I whispered. "Not now." I glanced at the screen on my hand, and my veins formed the word Melody. What was that supposed to be, Caller ID?

"Talk to the hand" just took on a whole new meaning.

I couldn't deal with explaining this to Melody or anyone else at the moment. I couldn't even explain it to myself. I ended the call and put my hand on vibrate as the truth of my situation hit me hard.

When kids make a face or cross their eyes, most parents tease that if they're not careful, their face will stay that way forever. Well, my parents tease if I'm not careful, I'll turn into one of my gadgets. I thought they were joking!

I fell back on my bed in disbelief as I attempted to process what had happened to me. I didn't need a new cell phone with a navigation system feature, because somehow, someway I had become a living, breathing, walking piece of technology.

I wasn't crazy, I was a freak.

A freak with a built-in GPS in my head, and my palm equipped with talking and texting capabilities. What else was I capable of? Taking pictures? Accessing the internet?

I rubbed my throbbing temples, then jerked back as a

mental image flashed in my mind's eye. What'd I do? What'd I touch? A table of contents like the main directory of my Electro Wave shot out my eyes in a holograph before me. I stared in shock, afraid to move, blink or breathe.

Finally, I reached before me to touch the main menu button. E-mail, voice mail, internet and photos were only the beginning of the list. I read on, sucking in a sharp breath. Language translation, infra-red night vision, heat sensors, wire-taps, sonar and x-ray features were also listed.

What kind of freaky cell phone did Mom give me?

I started to hyperventilate at the thought of that <u>thing</u> inside me. I couldn't breathe. It had to be a side effect of getting shocked by the space crystal, like when Spider Man got powers after getting bit by a genetically altered spider. Only, in my case, I was more like the Hulk. I couldn't control my actions. My powers seemed to have a mind of their own.

I blinked hard and the image disappeared. I had to pull it together, get a grip and figure out what to do. I did some yoga breathing for a good ten seconds, then searched my mom's closet and found a pair of old fingerless gloves, but that was only a temporary fix. I needed this to go away, like now!

My "unique" qualities were bound to interfere with my life. Kind of hard to make new friends if at a moment's notice my hand starts to vibrate.

Not to mention I'll look like a total spaz with my head tipping north, south, east and west. My nose twitching and lips puckering as I search for maps whenever someone asks for directions.

An even scarier thought occurred to me. What if I died from this electrical device inside me? Suddenly romance and social acceptance slid way down on my list of things to worry about. I had to find a way to reverse what had happened to me.

Or I might not have a life to look forward to at all.

"HEY," TREVOR SAID LATER THAT MORNING, DISTRACTING ME from my worries for a moment as he tossed the hacky sac he always carried from one hand to the other. Since he was into vintage eighties paraphernalia, maybe he wouldn't think my fingerless gloves were too weird.

Man, he looked good with his tight-fitting low slung jeans and brown graphic T-shirt hugging his well-muscled, super tall frame. I didn't care much for longish hair on guys, but he wore the look well. His wavy, brown hair with just a touch of blond highlights moved as he opened his locker and fished out the books he'd need for first period. The urge to run my fingers through the strands seized me. A whiff of his Axe body spray made me swoon, and I caught myself lifting a hand to touch him.

What was I doing?

He glanced at my hand with a funny look. I quickly fiddled with the combination on my lock, trying to regain what was left of my wits. I should be focusing on not dying, instead of drooling over some boy.

"Hey yourself, Trev, Trevo, The Trevster." Tell me I didn't just say that. Trevor made me so nervous. Like stomach gurgling, butt cheeks clenching, make a beeline to the bathroom kind of nervous. Talking to him was worse than taking a final exam.

His full lips twitched, but he didn't quite smile. "The Trevster?"

"It's better than the Trevinator." I snorted. Insert mental

forehead smack. I'd actually snorted. Like a pig looking for a treat. I'd settle for my dad's duct tape, but Trevo actually smiled. Well, sort of, but it was enough to make me smile back.

"I do love to tackle," he said in his deep shiver-inducing voice.

An image of him catching me and holding on tight sent chills to zip every which way throughout my body. I could feel data traveling all over the information highway. I froze--except for little electrical pulses. Maybe my micro chip or whatever was in there was frying my insides.

"Oh, God, I don't want to die," I said.

His forehead scrunched up. "Huh?"

I blinked, having forgotten he was still there. What had we been talking about? "Um, yeah. I mean, I would probably die if you tackled me, you being so big and all." I gestured with my hands. "Since I'm pretty fond of living, I guess I'll watch you play--watch the team, that is--from far away. Go football, right?" I pumped my fist in the air, feeling ridiculous.

"Right." His gaze landed on my hand still flailing about like a dimwitted gorilla.

Please let the bell ring now. I pressed my lips together and forced myself to lower my arm.

"What's wrong with your hand?" he asked.

My chest tightened. "Nothing! Nothing's wrong with my hand, why? Why do you ask?" My voice went up several octaves, causing plenty of curious looks from the crowded halls, and Mrs. Sweeny the guidance counselor to make a note in her ever present handy little notebook.

Oh, yeah, I'd be getting a call to her office in the near future. Looking forward to that conversation: 'Yes, Mrs. Sweeny, I'm fine. Fine as far as a regular well-oiled machine who could give Inspector Gadget a run for his money goes.'

Trevor held up his hands, drawing my attention back to him. He looked at me like I really had grown a third boob. Heart skipping a beat, my eyes darted down real quick to check. Whew. Two normal 34 A cups. Well, as normal as 34 A cups could be under the circumstances. Watch them start glowing next, giving new meaning to the words halogen headlights. I couldn't help wondering how long I had to live. What if I blew up? I needed to talk to Melody. She'd know what to do.

"You're wearing bandages," he said. "I just wondered if everything was okay." He took a step back. "Didn't mean to freak you out."

"Oh, that." I tried to control my breathing and act normal as I held my palms out in front of me. "Not bandages. I'm wearing gloves with no fingers, and I'm not freaked out. I have fall allergies, so I squeak a lot."

<u>Shut up now, Samantha. You're making things worse,</u> my brain said, but my mouth added, "Let's just say I'm starting a new trend, Trevo." I punched him on the arm. His cast iron arm. How much did this dude bench: a gazillion pounds? I shook my hand.

He studied me until I squirmed, then said in a quiet, intense voice, "You're kind of different, aren't you?"

"You could say that." I pushed my glasses up my nose-- I'd had to switch to fake ones since my vision was miraculously 20-20 now--and chewed the inside of my cheek. Where was that bell?

He gave my ponytail a tug. "Different is good." Slamming his locker closed, he backed away toward the door to our homeroom, tossing his hacky sac once more, his emerald-green eyes locked on mine.

Yeah, well, he could have being different. I'd had my fill and then some. Hey, wait a minute. My heart re-booted and ping-ponged against my ribs in hyper drive. Oh. My. God! Was Trevor "The Hottie" Hamilton flirting with Samantha "The Spaz" Granger? I just stood there like a dork watching him walk.

"See you in class, Samo." He smiled, then disappeared inside.

That smile definitely had flirting written all over it. I melted a little, but then reality set in. My pin-balling heart crashed like the hard drive on my old computer.

Trevor Hamilton finally noticed I was alive just when I found out I might die.

3

"SIDE EFFECTS"

Melody nudged my shoulder as she strolled up beside me, holding an armload of books, her rich mass of auburn curls falling to her waist. I wished I had hair like hers, and she wished she had teeth like mine. If we could combine the two of us, we'd have it made in the dating department.

Melody hated making more locker trips than necessary, so she carried as many books with her as possible. I couldn't blame her. Fate had <u>not</u> been kind to her this year, assigning Smelly Simon Van Alstyne as her locker neighbor. She'd already lost five pounds since she couldn't get out of making a locker stop before lunch. You couldn't pay her enough to eat by the time she hit the cafeteria.

At least he was helping her reach her goal of losing the ten pounds she said she'd put on since puberty. She was lucky. Puberty had given her curves. All it had given me was a monthly face full of zits.

"Samo? What was that about?" Melody's hazel eyes sparkled, and she smiled wide.

She hated her smile, but I thought she looked cute. And

real. Like a human being, not some fake Barbie doll. I'd seen enough of those back on the west coast.

"Wait, let me guess. I bet I know. I had a dream last night after you left, and it showed something dramatic was about to happen to you." She glanced toward our homeroom door. "I'm guessing this something has to do with Trevo?"

I thought about the smile. "Well, maybe, but never mind that."

"Are you feeling okay? Getting Trevor to like you was all you talked about this summer."

"Things change. I still like Trevor, but I've changed. I'm sure your dream was referring to these." I held up my white fingerless gloves.

"I know the eighties are making a comeback with leggings and skinny jeans, but fingerless gloves? Don't you think one era of that style is enough?"

"Long story. You're not going to believe what happened."

She grabbed my arm. "Don't tell me you got lost coming to school, too."

"If only. This is worse and ten times more embarrassing."

"Ladies, the bell rang ten seconds ago," Principal Norton growled from down the hall.

Sure, now the bell rings.

"Get to class, or I'll tell Melody's father to make you run extra laps in Phys Ed today." His beady little eyes reduced to slits.

"Yes sir," we both said, but the silent message we transmitted to each other screamed code red.

Major pow-wow later.

THAT AFTERNOON, SITTING IN GOVERNMENT, MELODY AND I chatted as we waited for Mr. Esposito to begin class. The social gods had smiled on me when they put Melody and Trevor in my fifth period. I sneaked a peek toward Trevor and thought maybe he had glanced my way, too. Quickly, I turned, but not before my face flushed bright crimson.

And not escaping the eyes of Gossip Queen, Alison Tucker. She looked at me and then at Trevor, then back to me. Back to Trevor! She gave me one last look while curling her lips into a cruel smirk.

I looked away, feeling my cheeks flush even hotter, and glanced at the wall of our social studies room. Ali's dad Congressman Tucker's campaign poster stared back at me. Perfectly coiffed blond hair and a smile that didn't quite reach his eyes sat right above the caption "Tough on crime, strong on safety."

"Did you guys hear the latest?" Alison blurted, pausing a beat to play out the drama.

Everyone went to her if they wanted the scoop on, well, anything. She even had a column in the school newspaper called "Ask Ali". Her dad wasn't the only one who seemed phony. Ali used anything she could to buy her friends. She had everyone fooled, but as an outsider, I could see right through her.

"Old news, Al," Melody chimed in. Speaking her mind and not giving a hoot what people thought was Mel's specialty. "Everyone knows about the kryptonite in the woods," she went on. "You're getting a bit rusty, there, Chica." She didn't like Ali any more than I did. Yet another thing I loved about Mel.

"Rusty? Don't think so," Ali snapped back. "The crystal is not kryptonite." Ali looked down her regal nose. "Like superheroes even exist. Get real." She filed her nails as though she was bored and shrugged.

"I wouldn't be sure about that," Simon said. "They say we only use ten percent of our brain. Do you honestly think in a universe this huge we're the only planet with life?"

I wished I had Simon's bravery. He didn't care what anyone thought about him.

"Whatever. I'm not even talking about the crystal anyway. I'm talking about the hikers who found it." Ali made eye contact with each one of us, not a platinum blond hair out of place. Her honey eyes glowed with anticipation, but we all knew she'd make us beg first.

I refused to cave. People who lived solely to make others' lives miserable just wasn't my scene. I'll bet she never once helped out with any of the local charities like I had with Gram back in L.A. I even helped out at the Salvation Army clothing store right here in town on weekends. It made me feel closer to Gram.

"Alright, I'll bite," Trevor said, leaning forward in his seat. "Who were the hikers?"

What is it about beautiful people? They all seemed to be drawn to one another like numbers on a calculator, but these two didn't add up. Couldn't they see they were so wrong for each other?

Ali batted her long lashes and leaned in to meet him half way, as though the two of them were having a private conversation. "Since you asked, Trevor, I won't keep you waiting. My sources say the twins, Bobby and Benny Burdick, were hiking through the woods when they found the glowing crystal," she divulged.

"Wait a minute. How could it be them? My mom said those two were grounded for shoplifting at the Nice-N-Easy," I interjected. I'd gotten a smile from Trevo only moments ago. Now that I was pretty sure I wasn't going to blow up, two could play this game.

Trevor leaned back a little and focused on me. "That's right, Sam. I'd forgotten about that. Good catch."

"Not really," Ali answered, recapturing his attention with an eyelash flutter for him and a smug smile for me.

I tried to act like she didn't bother me.

"Do you always listen to everything your parents say?" she asked me. "Oh, I'm so sorry. I forgot. Your parents split up, didn't they?" Her smiled looked sincere enough, but her eyes were sly and evil.

I slid down in my seat, wanting to pull all her perfect long lashes out, one by painful one.

"All I can say is thank God my parents are divorced," Maria Lopez popped her gum. "Major train wreck right from the start."

"Separated," I said quietly. "Mine are only separated."

"Oh, you poor thing. I can't imagine my parents ditching me and having to live with my grandmother. It must be awful. And those gloves...." She gave me a pity stare. "I heard about the warts. It has to be true, right? I mean why else would you wear those ... things." She stared at my gloves and grimaced.

"Shows what you know." Loyal to a fault, Melody came to my defense like a true best friend. "She doesn't have warts. The eighties are back and better than ever. And she lives with her mom now, so stuff it."

Ali opened her mouth, ready to fire off another sly remark.

"Get to the point, Ali," Trevor cut her off. He tossed his hacky sac right in front of her face as though daring her to make a comment to him.

He didn't look at me, but I felt the love from two rows

away. He'd stuck up for me, and <u>that</u> was huge. I glanced at Melody and mentally high-fived her.

"My mistake." Ali brushed a non-existent piece of lint off her mini-skirt. "Anyway, the Burdick boys are rule breakers. Sneaking out of the house and cutting through the woods is no surprise. Finding the crystal was a bonus."

"I heard it was radioactive." Melody looked skeptical. "Did they touch it?"

"They may be morons, but they're not stupid," Ali said. "Who would be dumb enough to do something like that?"

Forget blushing, my ears flamed hotter than an over-heated laptop as I thought about the charge that ran through me when I had been exactly that stupid! All eyes were still locked on the Gossip Queen as they waited for another juicy tidbit.

"Since the twins made the biggest discovery of the century, they're famous," Ali continued. "Their parents love being in the spotlight. Basically, the twins can do no wrong now."

Inside, I seethed.

I was the one who made the discovery; therefore, I should be the famous one. But I couldn't say anything because, as I said earlier, I <u>touched</u> it. I hoped no one could tell something was wrong with me, so long as I kept my gloves on. All in all, I appeared to be a normal teenage girl with odd taste in accessories. And I hadn't ruled out hope the incident could still have been a crazy dream.

"Did you hear me, Ms. Granger?" Mr. Esposito broke into my thoughts. "I said take out your book and turn to chapter three."

"G-Geography?" I croaked. "As in maps and statistics about places all over the world?"

This wasn't going to be pretty.

I swallowed hard. "I sort of studied up on geography over summer break," I lied, hoping no one would remember Sheriff Hamilton had to rescue me a few short weeks ago. I opened my book to chapter three, hoping nothing too weird would happen.

Mr. Esposito droned on and on about the importance of geographic concepts being central to a student's understanding of global connections. How we would expand our knowledge of diverse cultures, both historical and contemporary. And how we would use core geographic themes to public policy as we address issues of domestic and international significance.

So far so good. I let out a sigh of relief. Mr. Esposito loved to lecture, which meant spoon feeding us our education. Maybe I'd get through this after all.

"For instance, some day you might take a trip to South Africa. Do any of you even know what the cities in South Africa are?" he asked, clearly <u>not</u> expecting an answer. "Well, studying Geography will--"

Okay, maybe I wouldn't even last a day.

A groan slipped out of my mouth and that horrible pain ripped through my head, my vision blurring once more. My scalp tingled, my head tipped about, and the wheels in my brain churned until the answer popped into my mind, my headache and blurred vision lingering once again. Helpless to stop my annoying GPS voice from spitting out the answer, I stared at my book and refused to make eye contact with anyone.

I said all in one robotic tone: "There are nine cities in South Africa. Cape Town in Western Cape. Port Elizabeth in Easter Cape. East Condon in Eastern Cape. Durban in KwaZula-Natal. Pietermaritzburg in KwaZulu-Natal. Bloemfontein in Free State. Johannesburg in Gauteng. Pretoria in

Gauteng. East Rand in Gauteng. And Polokwane in Limpopo."

"Limp-whato?" someone asked.

"Limpopo," I repeated, mentally screaming for my alter ego to shut up. I felt mentally and physically drained the more I used my Electro Wave.

The room grew quiet as a TV on mute, and I could feel all eyes on me. I peeked up and saw several odd stares-- including Trevor--and my teacher at a loss for words.

"Well, I guess you really have done some studying, Ms. Granger." He nodded. "I'm impressed."

"I, um, always had a fascination with Africa?" my response came out more as a question, and a few snickers ricocheted about the room.

I looked like such a geek. Everyone knew if you were smart, you kept it quiet. It sure wasn't something you announced to the world, but the thing is I'm not a genius... or at least, I didn't used to be.

"Okay, then, moving on." Mr. Esposito pulled down a map and pointed to a random city without looking. "Say you wanted to travel here."

My left eye opened wide, the pupil expanding as the picture of the map zoomed in close enough for me to see. I jumped back as though I were watching a 3D movie. More heads turned my way, so I forced myself to sit still as my right eye snapped a picture--an actual picture--like my eyeball was a camera, all the while the teacher kept talking.

The picture saved digitally in a memory file in the many folds and grooves of my cerebrum. My brain cells processed the information, sending details to my nervous system in waves. I hoped no one heard the click and thanked good- ness I hadn't needed a flash. This was crazy, insane, ridiculous, I thought as I smoothed down my hair, which was now full of static electricity.

"You might want information like how big the city is, how many miles it would take to get there, the best route to-_"

Oh, please God, no. Make it stop. My head tipped southeast. My nose twitched--which had Melody rubbing hers--and my lips puckered.

This could not be happening, I thought, but then it did. I spit out in a monotone voice, "Hialeah, Florida. Population 217,141," then finished with precise directions from Blue Lake, NY to the southeast corner of the map.

Mr. Esposito whipped his head around to squint at the atlas, and then stared back at me in awe. "Well, I-I-I don't know what to say." He cleared his throat. "How on earth could you see the exact spot I was pointing to from that far away?"

"New glasses?" I said in question format again, clearing the hoarseness from my throat. My vocal chords actually ached.

"Next you'll tell us you know Morse Code," Ali scoffed, clearly not happy with me being the center of attention over her. Trust me; I wasn't any happier about it.

My spine snapped straight, and my brain accessed the online encyclopedia. Once it retrieved the information, it fired off the necessary technique to the motor neurons that carried the information straight to my tongue.

What now, I thought with dread as my tongue clicked out, "DAH,DIT,DAH,DAH ... DIT ... DIT,DIT,DIT,DIT." I started to sweat, feeling a whopper of a panic attack coming on, not to mention I now had several inflamed taste buds. At this point I'd prefer that third boob, even if it sprouted out on the center of my forehead. I was petrified to move.

God only knew what my body would do next.

"What did she say? Did she just call me a ditz?" Ali asked Mr. Esposito while looking at me in a phony wounded way.

"No," he said as though in shock. "She said y e s for yes in Morse code. DAH and DIT are the language of Morse code." He swiped a hand across his comb over which had flopped out of place. "I think we're looking at a phenomenon."

"I think--" Trevor started to say something, but then the bell rang.

I did <u>not</u> want to know what he had to say. At least school had ended for today. Just a soccer game left, but no one would be asking me for directions, I hoped. I should be fine until I could go home and work this whole thing out, but first things first.

I glanced at Melody, whose mouth still hung open, and knew I didn't need Morse code, dreams, ESP, or anything else for her to know exactly what I was thinking: We needed to talk, because something was seriously wrong with me.

4

GAME ON!

"What was that?" Melody shrieked as loud as one can shriek in a whisper voice. We were on the way to the soccer game, in the last row of a noisy, crowded bus.

I shoved my bag under my seat and tied my cleats. "I knew you wouldn't believe me."

"I didn't say I didn't believe you. You, oh keeper of secrets, are not yourself. Spill it." She threaded her long hair into a French braid and watched me, waiting patiently.

I took a deep breath, not knowing why I felt nervous. We'd been friends since the beginning of summer. I just didn't know what to think. But after all, if you couldn't trust your best friend, then who could you trust?

"You know how I got lost last night on the way home from your house?" I said.

She snorted. "Yeah, but after today's performance, I don't know how. What'd you do, take a crash course in navigation between then and now?"

"Sort of." I peeked up at her. "I turned on the GPS

feature of my phone and headed home, when I discovered the crystal."

"Crystal?" She took off her earrings and put them in her soccer bag. "Like a necklace?"

"The crystal, Mel. The kryptonite," I said in frustration.

"Excuse me. It's not my fault you talk in riddles." She sat back, crossing her arms.

"Sorry. I'm just scared, and I need your help. Everyone is going to think I'm a freak." I gave her a pleading look.

She rolled her eyes, but the anger had vanished and her lips tipped up a smidgen. "How exactly did you become the next, what was it Mr. Esposito said?"

"Phenomenon," I supplied.

"Right. Now, fill me in."

"Well, I discovered the crystal and--"

"Wait a sec, pause your gigabytes a minute and back up for us slower models. I thought the Burdick twins discovered the kryptonite." She pointed her finger in my face. "Before you try to correct me like know-it-all Ali, I'm not going to stop calling it kryptonite. If it really is from outer space, then Superman might be right behind to rescue me."

"Nice thought, but somehow, I doubt it."

"Crazier things have happened." She flicked my glove.

I flexed my hand. It felt normal, but I was afraid to take off my glove and see what was there. "The Burdick boys do not deserve to be famous. They found the crystal after I discovered it, but I can't tell anyone because I am more of an idiot than they are."

"I could have told you that." She laughed, and I smacked her on the arm. "You actually saw the krypto up close?"

"Oh, I more than saw it." I swallowed hard. "I, um, oh God, here goes. I touched the stupid thing and got zapped."

"No way!" She gaped at me, looking comical. It took a lot to shock Mel.

"Yes way." I nodded.

"What happened? Did you tell your mom? Did you have to go to the hospital? What?"

"Nothing. I was thrown twenty feet and knocked out cold, but I woke up fine. Well, not exactly fine, but I wasn't hurt."

"Okay. What do you mean 'not exactly fine'?"

"Did you see me today? I'm surprised my head didn't spin around, because I swear, something has possessed me."

She giggled. "So you got ridiculously smart overnight and dominated the class by answering every question. That's hardly 'Exorcist' worthy." She hoisted one shoulder. "Nerd worthy, definitely. If you want to hear freaky, one time my little brother--"

I slipped off the glove and held my hand out before her.

"Wow. A hand. Big whoop. It looks normal to me, except for that rash. Or do you seriously have warts?" She reached out and touched one of my brail bumps which took my phone off sleep mode. My skin turned transparent once again, glowing the same bright blue-green. "Eeek! What is that?" Her eyes bugged and she yanked her hand back as though I were contagious, scrambling as far away from me as she could.

"It's just my hand." I reached out, but she swatted my arm away.

"Don't touch me. That is <u>not</u> just a hand." She studied my face. "And, what have you done with my best friend?"

"Come on, Mel. I'm still me, I'm just ... different." I leaned closer to her.

"Stay back. That's what you want me to believe, but I've

read enough of my brothers' comics. You aliens think you're so much smarter than humans." She thrust her palms up between us. "I know karate. Give me back my friend, and I won't hurt you."

"Knock it off." This time I swatted her hands away. "I am Sam, you ditz."

"Prove it." She poked me, then jumped back even further.

I huffed out a breath. "You sleep with Mr. Fuzzy Wuzzy."

Mel frowned. "I told you never to repeat that."

"Sometimes you suck your thumb in your sleep."

She gasped. "I do not."

"And you have an ingrown toenail on the big toe of your right foot."

"I believe you. Just stop talking. Someone might hear."

A head popped up over the seat in front of us. "Hear what? What are you guys yelling about?" Maria asked, blowing a huge pink bubble, then getting it stuck in her silky, flat-ironed black hair. "Oh." She grabbed the ends and started scraping the gum out with her manicured black-painted fingernail.

Thankful for the distraction, I shoved my illuminated hand under my thigh. "You just missed a naked guy dart out of the woods on the side of the road."

"For real?" Maria's dark brown eyes grew huge, her gummy hair forgotten.

"Oh, yeah," Melody said, not taking her eyes off me, "Freakiest thing I've ever seen."

Maria disappeared as quickly as she'd popped up. Within minutes, all eyes were glued to the windows on the lookout for Non-Existent Au-natural Nature Boy.

Once I was sure no one was looking, I pulled my hand

from under my leg and tugged on my glove. "That is my Electro Wave."

"Get out!" Mel sputtered.

"This is about as out there as it gets. When you called me this morning and I didn't answer, it was because my phone started ringing in my hand. I'm not an alien; I'm some type of teen machine."

Her face looked frozen in shock.

"I'm serious. When I woke up from getting knocked out, I couldn't find my cell phone anywhere, but I knew exactly how to get home. Then this morning when I knew the exact directions to tonight's game and my hand started ringing, I knew I was different."

"How'd you know it was me?" she whispered, looking dazed.

"Trust me; my brail bumps and neon see-through skin is just the start of what my hand can do. My veins got all tangled and your name popped up in my Caller ID."

"That's messed up."

"Ya think?" I grabbed her hands, and this time, she didn't flinch. "Please tell me you believe me. I can't go through this alone."

She stared at me for a long moment. "Was there ever any doubt? Of course I believe you. You're my best friend--even though you're totally give me the creeps!"

"I love you." I gave her a quick hug.

"Me too." She hugged me back. "It's kind of cool you have the latest upgraded cell phone literally at your fingertips."

I scowled.

"Okay, maybe not, but look at the bright side." She held up her finger. "No pun intended, I swear." I rolled my eyes this time, and she continued, "Your grades are bound to improve, and you won't have to worry about getting lost anymore. At least Trevor stuck up for you today."

My gaze met hers. "You caught that?"

"I think he likes you."

One short day ago that would have given me the same buzz as when I'd first opened my Electro Wave. But today, everything was different. My life had changed drastically, and I was afraid I'd never get the old me back. "I doubt he's going to like my ringing, vibrating, clicking little quirks. They're not exactly cute material."

"I don't know. I heard someone in the locker room say they thought your gloves were adorable."

"Only in Blue Lake would someone think these gloves were adorable."

"No kidding." She laughed. "What are you going to do?"

"I have no clue. My parents would go psycho on me. With those scientists already here to study the crystal, I'm sure they'd lock me up in a lab right beside it. I can't risk anyone finding out my secret until I figure out a way to reverse my uniqueness."

"That's one word for it." She snorted.

"Mel..."

"Sorry." She rubbed her hands together. "Trevor can't see your uniqueness. He's definitely into you, and you don't want to blow it."

"You really think he's into me?" I latched onto hope.

"I know so, but don't get excited. I saw the look on his face when you started acting like a brainiac with Tourettes. He looked--"

"Disgusted? I knew it. He thinks I'm weird, doesn't he?" I dropped my face into my hands. This was starting out to be the worst year ever.

"Calm down." She patted my back. "I was going to say confused. Like he was trying to figure you out. We all were."

"What do I do?"

"Well." She thought for a minute. "I know. No one knows you that well, so make them think you have a photographic memory like your Gram." She smiled wide while nodding. "Yeah, I like it. That could work."

"You watch too many movies." I giggled, shaking my head. "But you might be on to something."

"My mom always says I should write books because I have a wild imagination."

"Good. Then write me out of this mess, please. Cuz the novelty has worn off big-time."

"I'm on it."

The bus pulled up to White Peak Junior High, and I stepped off feeling slightly better. I wasn't alone anymore. And Mel was in my corner. I just had to stay out of trouble and get through tonight's game, then retreat to my room to research possible ways to reverse these side effects. So why couldn't I shake the bizarre feeling my troubles had only begun?

I MIGHT BE MELODY'S BEST FRIEND, AND I MIGHT BE LIKE another daughter to her dad, but I was definitely not one of his star players. On the soccer field, he was all coach.

Mel was a starter. She was a right wing with an awesome hook shot, and Maria was our powerhouse striker, front and center. As a duo, they were unstoppable.

Sometimes I got jealous. Mel and I were so tight and shared everything, except a talent for soccer. I played backup goalie, but rarely got to go in. No matter what I did,

I couldn't stop a ball, even with Mel helping me all summer.

I glanced at the stands and waved to my mom. She sat right by Simon who came to all our games to keep stats for Coach Stuart. Mom waved back distractedly, looking worried as she talked on her cell phone. Had to be work. Still, I was glad she'd made it.

Back in California, my dad was the one who went to my games. I missed checking out the bleachers and knowing he was there looking as disheveled as ever with his messy brown hair, wrinkled suit and crooked glasses. I grinned, picturing his humongous smile, same as always. Mr. Wally Granger was my biggest fan, like only a father can be. My grin dimmed. All that had changed now. He'd call me later, but it wouldn't be the same.

With an aching heart, I turned back to watch the game from the bench, then did a double take. My breath hitched like a hiccup on my iPod, and my palms broke out in a sweat, dampening the gloves on my hands.

Never in a million years had I expected Trevor Hamilton to show up. He must be cutting football practice, but why? Just to watch our game? I risked a peek to see who he was watching out on the field, and nearly peed my pants. His gaze wasn't on the field. It was locked on me!

Ohmigod, Ohmigod, Ohmigod, what should I do? Should I wave? Should I say something? Should I--

"Samantha, I said you're in," Coach Stuart barked, and I fell right off the bench.

"What?" I scrambled to my feet, feeling like I was going to throw up. *Why me, why here ... why now?*

"Debbie sprained her wrist blocking that last shot." Debbie was our starting goalie, and well, awesome. No way could I live up to that.

"But...."

"Take a breath. You'll do fine, kiddo. Now hustle. Your team needs you." He slapped me on the back, propelling me out on the field. Out to my doom. Out to my complete and utter humiliation.

Why oh why did Trevor have to choose this game to go to?

5

RECALCULATING

I jogged out to the goal. Slipping in front of the net, I faced the players on the field and bounced on the balls of my feet in a ready position. I wanted Trevor to think I knew what I was doing.

I channeled my inner Gram determination and focused on the game, refusing to let anything distract me. If I could get through this last quarter without making a fool of myself, I'd be golden. Today was turning out to be a nightmare.

Melody and Maria moved the ball down the field as though the two were one, lining up the perfect shot. Mel faked left, then nailed the ball with a fabulous right hook, sending it sailing in Maria's direction. Maria jumped high and whacked the ball hard with her forehead, scoring in the far right corner of the net.

The crowd went wild.

Up until this moment, White Peak had been kicking our butt five to zip. Maybe this first score was our chance to turn things around. The ball headed in my direction. Oh, God, maybe not. I'd almost forgotten I was now our team's only hope as goalie.

The White Peak girls were big. And mean. What did they put in the water out here? I took a breath and reminded myself I could do this. I needed to have faith, have hope, have confidence ... or have a heart attack.

My eyes traveled back and forth, watching the ball, watching every player's move. When the striker in the center hit the ball, a calm settled over me. My camera-lensed eyes zeroed in on the shot, then locked in place. My sensory neurons carried the information to my cerebellum, and just like that I knew exactly where the ball was going to enter the net.

My motor neurons shot the proper response message down my spinal cord to my arms and legs. As though my body had a will of its own, I leapt in the air, thrusting my hands above my head and blocked the shot from the upper left corner. Landing hard, I rolled to my tingling feet to face a stunned crowd, the pulse of my racing heart throbbing in my fingertips.

Everyone sat in utter silence, staring at me as though I'd morphed into a different person. In a way, I had.

My mom yelled, "Yeah, honey! That's my girl!"

The crowd surged to their feet in a roar of applause, and I smiled wider than I ever had. I was exhausted and still not quite myself, but this was more like it--a side effect I could get used to. A newfound confidence filled me, and the rest of the game went off better than anyone could have expected. We not only beat White Peak, we annihilated them. There wasn't a shot I couldn't stop thanks to the pinpoint accuracy of my GPS brain.

My team rushed me in the goal, lifting me in the air and patting me on the back, with Mel giving me a knowing look and a big high-five. When they put me on my feet and finally backed off, I started to head over to my mom, but stopped in my tracks. Trevor walked in my direction, his thumbs hooked in his jeans pockets, his eyes locked on mine.

Okay, back to freaking out. I bit my bottom lip as I watched him slowly walk toward me, looking like an Abercrombie ad--his hair blowing in the fall breeze, his muscles bunching and flexing with his every step. A strange heat flooded my body, and my limbs grew heavy. I swayed slightly and felt my breathing deepen as the pressure bubbled within me.

I seriously felt like I was going to explode.

"Great game, Samo," he said as he reached me, flipped his hair to the side, and tossed his hacky sac.

I snatched it out of the air before he could, faster than a high speed internet connection. I tried to disguise the effect he had on me, but that didn't stop my hormones from continuing to skyrocket. I held the hacky sac out before him, feeling confident and ignoring the slight numbness in my hands and feet.

"Impressive." He took the sac from me and our fingers brushed.

I felt a tingle straight through my glove and swallowed hard, breaking out in a sweat from the heat surging within me. Snatching my hand back, I took a huge breath. I couldn't get enough air.

"Thanks. I've been practicing," I said. A nervous giggle slipped out.

His gaze ran over the length of me. "You looked good out there."

"Thanks. I've been practicing," I said again. "But you

know that because I just said that." Duh. Time to change the subject, Samo. "What's up?"

"Not much." He shoved his hands in his pockets and, for the first time since I'd met him, looked uncomfortable. "There's something I've been wanting to ask you."

Trevor nervous? I couldn't imagine him nervous about anything. Unless ... Was he going to ask me out right here, right now? My internal pressure cooker within was building to a level that made my eyes cross. Something inside me felt like it was going to snap, literally.

He cleared his throat. "I was wondering--"

"Owww," I howled like a wolf and grabbed my throbbing head, my cortex overloaded with information from my five senses, and my pituitary gland making an excessive amount of hormones. A loud pop and a flash of a bright white light followed by a phone number I didn't recognize ran through my mind's eye.

"You okay?" he asked.

"I'm fine," I lied. My adrenal glands kicked into gear, releasing adrenaline, and shooting extra power into my muscles. My body jerked forward. "Wow," I said as my feet started walking in the direction of the woods. No matter how many times I told them to stand still, they wouldn't stop moving.

"Hey, where are you going?"

I wish I knew, I wanted to shout, but the funny thing was I had no clue. My legs moved as though they had a will of their own, carrying me in some anonymous direction like my body was locked on autopilot mode. It terrified me, but didn't really surprise me. I just chalked it up to the list of freakishly weird things that were happening to me since last night.

Not about to let my own legs get in the way of this

conversation, I said, "Walk with me? I've got a nasty headache. Besides, my mom will kill me if I keep her waiting. She's got some work function to go to. You were saying?" I asked, but my legs chose that moment to pick up the pace. Double-time.

"I can give you a ride on my bike if you want." He jogged to catch up to me.

Of course I wanted to! But since my body wasn't cooperating with my brain, stepping onto the pegs on the back of his bike was pretty much impossible at the moment.

"My mom won't let me ride on a bike with a strange boy. Not that I think you're strange, I just mean, with boys she hasn't met." I winced. That sounded unbelievably lame.

"Do you have to walk so fast?" his deep voice rumbled, and his brows shot up into his hairline as he looked at my legs. "And like that?"

With my arms flailing about to keep my balance, I had to look like a majorette in a marching band. All I needed was a baton. I started waving to everyone I passed in hopes of disguising my awkwardness. "Victory dance," I said, nearly out of breath.

"Oh-kay." He frowned and rubbed his jaw, looking as though he were making his mind up about something. Probably me.

People all around us started joining in, looking much cooler than I did. Everyone danced and cheered in the parking lot, shouting that Blue Lake Junior High rocked.

I stared at him, wondering if I'd made him change his mind about whatever he wanted to ask me. He just shrugged like it was no big deal, but I swear a spark of something passed between us.

"Anyway," he said. "I wanted to ask you--"

"There you are, Trevor," Annoying Ali said out of breath.

"I've been looking for you everywhere. Your dad's here, and he's not happy. He sent me to find you. Something about football practice." Ali smiled sweetly at Trevor while at the same time, amazingly, smirking evilly at me.

He pulled away and I could see that wall of his going back up. He tried to look bored, like he could care less. Then his gaze shot to mine and, for a second, a flash of disappointment crossed his face, but then it vanished. "Guess I'd better go before my old man has a coronary. Catch up with you later?"

"Sure. Whatever." I hoisted a shoulder as though it was no big deal, not wanting to seem desperate. But I couldn't help clenching my fist, accidentally hitting the voice mail button as he walked away with Annoying Ali. My hand began to vibrate.

Ali looked way too chummy. If he asked her whatever he had planned to ask me, I would die. But apparently, I couldn't stick around to find out. Stupid, stupid legs!

"Sam, where are you going?" Melody asked. "Hey, wait up, I'm talking to you. And quit waving. People are staring."

"I know, and I'm sorry, but I can't stop."

"Why not?" She jogged along beside me and kept trying to grab my arms.

"Literally. I can't stop." I almost hit her in the head, but she ducked at the last second.

"Oh." She winked. "Right." Giving me a thumbs-up, she marched beside me until we were far enough away from everyone. "I think you're in the clear." She glanced around to make sure the focus was off us. "Do whatever you have to, and I'll cover for you. I'll tell your mom you're coming to my house to celebrate, but it's over a five mile walk home, you know."

"Thanks for reminding me."

"Hey, that's what a sidekick is for. Remember come to my house whenever you're done with wherever you end up."

Now, there was a disturbing thought. Where would I end up? At this point, I didn't have a clue. Somehow I didn't think a simple pair of ruby red slippers would take me home. Like Dorothy, I was helpless to do anything but follow the yellow brick road and see where it took me.

Look out Oz, here I come.

WHAT FELT LIKE HOURS LATER, I FINALLY ARRIVED AT OLD Lady Lipowitz's house. The woman had to be ninety, but still lived alone. Why didn't she just call 911? I had so many questions, but no one to go to for answers.

I knocked on the door for a whole minute. Nothing. I searched the premises, but still no Mrs. Lipowitz. I heard a noise coming from the garage, so I went to investigate. Just before I reached the entrance, a cat launched itself out of a trash can by the door, knocking it over. I flinched. I didn't know why I was chosen to help Mrs. Lipowitz, but I couldn't leave the poor woman until I found out. I went back to the front door of the house and turned the knob.

It opened.

"Hello? Is anyone home?" I asked.

Again, no answer.

I went inside. The place was dark and smelled like oatmeal cookies. I turned on a light ... and stopped short. Mrs. Lipowitz was lying on the floor in her kitchen, not moving. What was I supposed to do? The Girl Scout in me knelt beside her and felt for a pulse. She was still alive, just unconscious. Her hand was burned. That must be why she needed help. She was too old to drive herself to the hospital, and I'd heard she'd been widowed for a long time now.

When I touched her head, her eyes opened. "What happened?"

"Uh, you burned your hand and something knocked you out, I guess. Don't worry, I have a cell. I'll call 911 for you."

"I remember calling 911 when I heard a loud pop and saw a bright flash of white light. The next thing I knew, my phone exploded and I don't remember anything else. You're an angel, honey. Who are you?" she asked in a raspy voice. "I can't see anything without my glasses."

Thank you god of small miracles. "Hang on a sec, I'm on the phone," I lied to buy myself some time. I was no angel, I was just a girl. An unusual girl, I'd give her that, but I still didn't know what I had to do with any of this.

I slipped off my soccer glove and dialed 911. After filling them in on Mrs. Lipowitz's condition, I disconnected, even though they told me to stay on the line. Wouldn't that look cute if the ambulance showed up and caught me talking into my hand?

I couldn't tell her who I was because Melody told my mom I got a ride home. Mrs. Lipowitz's house was not on the way home. And Trevor thought I had to ride home with my mom. If word got out I'd helped Mrs. Lipowitz, people would start asking questions.

My parents would have me committed if the special team of scientists didn't lock me up first. What if this happened again? I didn't know how or why I had been summoned, but like Spider Man had Spidey Sense and could tell when people were in trouble, apparently I had GPS sense.

I didn't know what triggered it or why I was sent to help this particular woman and not others, but one thing I did know. If my GPS sensor went off again, I would be sent to the rescue whether I liked it or not. There was only one thing I could do.

Come up with a disguise just in case.

"Don't worry, Mrs. Lipowitz, help is on the way," I said, hearing real sirens--not the ones in my head--off in the distance. I got up and headed to the door to escape.

"Wait. You never did tell me who you were," she said in a feeble voice. Figured she'd remember. She might be old, but her mind was still razor sharp.

I sighed, not wanting to accept what was happening to me, but obviously I didn't have a choice. I didn't have much time before emergency crews arrived, either, so I said the first thing that popped into my mind.

"Just call me Hard Wired."

Melody had no idea how close to the truth she was when she'd joked about being my sidekick. Apparently, I'd been re-routed on a path of no return, even if I was a reluctant participant. But there was nothing I could do about it.

Whether I liked it or not, a superhero had just been born.

6

SUPER WHAT?

Mel's house was only one block away, thank God. I felt like I had the flu, I was so tired. I couldn't deal with any more excitement for one day.

I broke through a clearing in the woods, right by the Salvation Army, intending to stop and tell them to put me on the schedule this weekend. Sucking in a breath, I froze. There was Trevor with his back to me as he disappeared inside with Congressman Tucker, carrying big boxes of used clothing.

Ali's used clothing.

She stood by her dad's gold metallic Mercedes, not lifting a finger to help. I shook my head, but I couldn't help focusing on that fabulous car. My heart sank. My dad drove a Prius--let's just say he was Mr. Practical with a capital P. Forget donating material things, my dad was into giving homemade things like the organic brownies he made for my Girl Scout troop's pledge drive. His heart might be made of gold. His ideas ... not so much.

I tried to slip away without Ali seeing me.

"Well, look who it is. Surfer Girl. Oops, silly me. I meant, Samantha Granger. Nice victory dance, by the way." She smiled all innocent like, but it didn't reach her eyes. "What are you doing here?"

I shrugged. "I help out."

"Of course you do."

"You should give it a try sometime," I said, then muttered under my breath, "It might take the edge off your horns."

She looked bored. "It's not really my thing, but I donate plenty. You know, for people who come here." Her eyes narrowed a fraction. "Like you."

I ignored her sly jab. "I thought Trevor's dad was bringing him home from the game."

"Sheriff Hamilton got called away on some 911 call, so he asked my dad to give Trevor a ride home." Ali's smiled turned catlike. "Trevor jumped at the chance to ride with me."

"Really? I heard his dad was forcing him to do community service as punishment for missing football practice." I hadn't heard any such thing, but I was tired of not standing up to her subtle insults.

"Look around you," she said, all traces of subtlety gone. "You can't compete. Why don't you save yourself the heartache and give up."

"And miss all this? Why, that would make my heart ache even more." I clenched my teeth, angry at letting her get to me, then marched away with renewed energy before Trevor could come out and see me.

Ali's tinkling laughter stung my ears for the block.

A while later, after Melody insisted I forget about Annoying Ali, I filled her in on everything that had happened.

"Stop laughing, would ya?" I said as I glanced around her bedroom. Pictures of David Beckham covered every inch of her walls. He wasn't "Trevor cute," but he was still drool worthy.

"I can't help it. Hard Wired?" She snorted. "That's just too funny."

"Yeah, well, the name's a work in progress. I had to come up with something. Old Lady Lipowitz wouldn't stop asking. I still don't know how I ended up there, or if it'll happen again. I need to be prepared next time, so help me create a disguise."

"Fine. Move over and let the master work." She plopped down and grabbed her laptop from me.

"Master? Puh-lease!" I eyed her soccer shorts and T-shirt. "Your sense of style looks great in a locker room. And you wonder why Scott Randolph thinks of you as one of the guys."

"What guys do you know that have to wear a sports bra? And you should talk, Ms. Constant Ponytail. Can I help it I like sports?" She wound a long auburn curl around her finger as she scanned her computer.

"I don't always wear a ponytail." Did I? I frowned. "And I like sports too, but I don't live in my jersey and cleats."

"You're not the only one on a mission this year. Once Scott sees I'm better at handling a ball than he is, he'll be hooked." She gave a mischievous smile that crinkled her cheeks. "I just thought of something. Scott is Trevor's best friend."

"I know," I said slowly.

"And I'm your best friend."

"Right. So?"

"We both know Trevor likes you, so share the wealth."

"We don't know for sure he likes me. He never asks

anyone out." Mel's words suddenly registered, and I scrunched up my face. "Wait a minute ... you want me to share Trevor?"

"No! For such a brainiac, you're really slow in the guy department." I tried to smack her with a pillow, but she ducked in time. "I want you to set up a double date."

"Date! But he hasn't even asked me out."

"Ask him out."

Total panic plowed through me. I twisted her white and black checkered fleece throw and gnawed the inside of my cheek. "I can't."

"You wuss." She yanked the blanket from my fingers and tossed it over my head.

"I am not a wuss," I said, emerging from beneath. "I don't want to be shot down if you're wrong."

"Fine, we'll play it your way, but I'm determined to prove I'm right. Trevor Hamilton has the hots for you, quirks or no quirks."

"Speaking of quirks, can we get back to my problem of a disguise please?"

"Relax, I've got it covered. My mom made all the costumes for the cheerleaders this year."

"I do not want to look like a cheerleader."

"Don't worry, I'm on it." Melody's fingers flew as she Googled superheroes, fashion, newest styles, celeb teens, and disguises without much success. I did the same internally without any luck, either.

"What about this one?" Mel asked, pointing at the tutu displayed on her laptop screen.

"Get real. When I get 'the call,' I can't stop walking. It's going to be kind of hard to change into that along the way without falling."

"Don't change. Strip."

"What?" I gaped at her as though she were the one from outer space.

"I mean, wear your costume beneath your clothes every day so all you have to do is strip."

I grinned wide. "You're a genius."

She shrugged, but her grin equaled mine. "I try. We're both smart, capable girls. We ought to be able to come up with something." She chewed her lip and looked pensive, then her face lit up. "I've got an idea. Let's look at my brothers' comic books. I bet we find a ton of cool costume ideas in there."

Mel raced into her twin brothers' bedroom and returned seconds later with her arms loaded. We sat for a good ten minutes pouring over every page of every comic book.

"Whoever writes these things is the most chauvinistic dude in the universe. There are barely any female superheroes." Mel tossed the comic book on her bed.

"No kidding. The few they show do not look realistic. There's no way I could pull off those measurements even if I wanted to, thank you very much," I said.

"Bummer. What are you gonna do? You can't wear anything 'Sam' would wear, and if you borrow anything of mine, everyone will think I'm Hard Wired."

I thought about that and started to worry until a brilliant idea came to me. "I'm sure we can find something at the Salvation Army. People just dropped off tons of new stuff."

"Come on. My parents won't be home for a while. Let's ride bikes there. You can use my brother's. I can't wait to see what we find."

AN HOUR LATER BACK AT MEL'S HOUSE, I TRIED ON MY costume. "This is perfect," I said, excitement rippling through me.

Mel had gone all undercover operation on me, carrying out our "mission impossible" in secret. Tourism in town had picked up since the crystal hit Blue Lake and the scientists had shown up. Tons of people I'd never seen were in the store, and Simon had even made an appearance. Mel suggested we walk in separately. I searched the clothing racks and she searched the shoe department. The result...

One totally cute superhero!

I wore a tight, sparkly pink and purple jumpsuit with knee-high black boots and even a little matching mask and cape, like someone had cleaned out their playhouse. Lucky me.

Mel tilted her head and looked me over from every angle, then clapped her hands. "You look adorable."

"Thanks." I checked out my reflection in her bedroom mirror. With my hair down, glasses off, and mask on, I looked nothing like Sam, reminding me of why I needed this costume. I sighed. "This whole thing is ridiculous. I'm no superhero."

Mel gave me a quick hug. "Don't stress. Let's check out the social networks? Do some snooping and see if anyone knows anything about Hard Wired."

"Cute or not, I'm hoping I will never have to wear this costume," I said as I pulled my normal clothes on over my disguise. "Maybe the whole thing will just go away. I don't want to be a superhero."

"Apparently, you don't have a choice. Until your powers go away, can't we have fun with them? Nothing exciting ever happens around here. I wanna be your sidekick."

"Being a superhero is scary. One rescue was enough for

me." I had to put an end to the sidekick idea before Mel got too excited. Once she got excited, there was no stopping her.

Mel didn't say a word, but I could see the wheels in her head spinning ... literally. I rubbed my eyes to erase the x-ray pictures they had snapped of Mel's thought processes.

"You want to get something to eat? I'm starved." I headed out to her kitchen, feeling more at home in her house than mine. I practically lived there. Her parents had even started calling me their sixth child.

"Any left over pizza in the fridge?" Mel asked.

"Nope, but I just placed an order. Should be here any minute."

Her face puckered up. "Huh?"

I tapped my skull. "Ordered online. Gotta love being hard wired. At least it has some perks."

"Wanna sneak one of my dad's mocha lattes?" Mel wagged her brows as she scooted by me.

"Are you crazy? Your dad will know."

"We're talking about my dad, not your mom. Believe me, he doesn't count his iced coffees, and he's always well-stocked. She snatched a latte from the fridge and shuffled the bottles around just in case. Twisting the top off, she took a sip, grimacing a little. "A cup of Java a day keeps the crazies away. Want some?" She held the bottle out to me.

"Gee, let me think ... no!"

"I repeat, wuss!" She giggled. We loved teasing each other, but knew it was all in good fun.

"I told you, I am not a wuss, ya delinquent."

"Okay, goody-goody--what's Mom call it--oh, yeah ... prude." Mel took another tentative sip and grimaced again. She dumped the coffee in the sink on a shudder. "How do people like that stuff? Never mind, help me stash this bottle before I get busted." Mel wrapped the bottle in a paper bag and buried it in the bottom of the trash can out in the garage. She'd just come back in when the pizza guy showed up.

I paid him with my allowance and set the box on the counter. After Mel and I both inhaled two slices, I thought of something. "Shouldn't your parents be home by now?"

Mel's parents were constant taxis and never at the same event together. Her dad had coached our soccer game earlier and had promised to celebrate tonight after he got home from picking up Mel's little sister, Annabella, from dance class. While Mel's mom had been busy picking up Mel's brother, Joey, from football practice and taking the twins, Tyler and Tanner, to karate.

I personally got dizzy just thinking about how they kept it all straight ... but I loved every chaotic second of it. My house was way too quiet, as though everything inside had been put on mute permanently.

Mel glanced at the tree-shaped clock, sitting on the black bear lamp beneath the stuffed deer head in their Adirondack-themed family room. Her dad liked to hunt, which was pretty much why my mother never accepted an offer to have dinner with them.

"Huh, that's weird," Mel said. "Don't you love how we get in trouble if we're even one minute late, yet they can be an hour late with no phone call. That's not right." She picked up her cell and had just dialed her mother when the front door burst open.

7

KNOCK KNOCK, WHO'S THERE?

"I cannot wait until you get your license, Melody," Mrs. Stuart said as she carried in bags of KFC and plopped them on the kitchen counter in the Stuart household. Tanner and Tyler lunged for the bag at the same time, but Mel's mom caught them by the backs of their white karate Gi's, loosening their belts. "I don't think so, boys. And you," she thrust a finger at Joey, "In the shower. You reek to high heaven."

"Gee thanks, Mom." Joey's face turned red as he glanced at me, then bolted up the stairs two at time. Mel sang, 'Joey's got a cru-ush, Joey's got a cru-ush,' keeping time with his every step like the bass on a CD track.

I smacked her on the arm as her mom admonished, "Why do you have to embarrass him like that?"

"Because it's fun. He stole my magazine again this month, the little dork."

"Melody Ann Stuart, that's not nice," she snapped, then turned around to pull the paper plates out of the pantry.

Annabella came in, twirling around the kitchen in her

fluffy tutu, looking adorable. I smiled at her as I grabbed the napkins and silver. "Add an extra twirl for me, 'kay?"

She giggled and bowed gracefully, then twirled out of the room to change for dinner.

"Mom, where's Dad?" Mel asked, getting up and pouring the drinks. "Wasn't he supposed to pick up Bella?"

"He got an EMT call and had to ride along in the ambulance, which is exactly why I need you to get your license, ASAP. Juggling everyone's schedules is too much for one person."

"Even if I was old enough, you can't expect me to drive Dad's hunk of junk. That is not a car. It's social suicide! Back me up on this one, Sam."

"Huh, what? Oh, right. Yeah, I guess," I muttered, half listening. I couldn't get Mr. Stuart's emergency call out on off my mind.

Could it have been Mrs. Lipowitz? What did she tell him? Had he figured out who I was? My stomach hurt; I couldn't eat if I tried. Oh, God, was I getting sick? The instruction manual in a file in another fold of my cerebellum had said a glowing red button would indicate a virus. I glanced down at the only button I had ... my belly button. Phew. No red light. Must be nerves. At least I hoped that's all it was. I was still struggling to get through reading the ginormous manual with my mind's eye. Not an easy task.

Maybe I needed Cyclops glasses.

"Honey, I'm ho-ome," Mr. Stuart sing-songed as he sailed through the door and gave his wife a bear hug.

I stifled a sad smile. It had been so long since I'd seen my parents embrace, I wondered if I ever would again. I needed to call Gram. She always cheered me up.

"Just in time. Now, there's a surprise," Mrs. Stuart said on a laugh, then gave him a quick peck on the lips. "Better grab a drumstick before the human garbage disposals get down here."

"Good idea," he snagged the biggest drumstick from the bucket, an iced coffee from the fridge--Mel shot me an I-told-you-so look--then he sat at the table. "Hey, Sam, glad to see you made it. You heard the little lady, dig in before the animals have at it. But save some room for cake. We've got some celebrating to do over our new starting goalie."

"Seriously?" I asked, stunned, forgetting about Mrs. Lipowitz for a moment. This was something I'd wanted so badly, but had never been able to achieve ... until now.

"Debbie is out for the season, and you deserve it after the way you played this afternoon. I didn't know you had it in you."

"You and me both," Mel said, snickering. "Sam's become good at a lot of things recently. You should see her in Social Studies class. Mr. Esposito calls her a phenomenon."

I stomped her foot under the table, and she bit back a groan, then mouthed, 'sorry.'

"It's nothing," I said through a bright smile and locked jaw. "I just brushed up on my geography over the summer is all."

"And apparently your physics as well. I've never seen someone so accurate on covering the goal before. It was like you knew exactly where the ball was going to enter the net at all times. Uncanny," he said, looking pensive.

"What can I say, I love school. Thanks for giving me this chance, Coach," I said, relieved when he stopped staring off into space and refocused on me. "I promise I won't let you down." I was pretty sure I could keep that promise since my 'uniqueness' wasn't going away anytime soon. I helped myself to a piece of chicken.

"Oh, honey, don't you want to take your gloves off?" Mrs. Stuart asked.

"Uh, no, my hands are freezing, but my gloves are clean. I promise." My laugh sounded strange to my own ears. Desperate to take the focus off me, I asked hesitantly, "I, um, heard you went out on a 911 call, Coach. Anything serious?"

"Old Lady Lipowitz burned her hand making cookies. I've told that woman a million times she should take her daughter up on living with her. Ever since she was widowed, she's more stubborn than ever."

"So she's all right then?"

"Oh, she's fine. Lucky, though. Someone broke into her garage and tore through some old boxes. Probably a bunch of kids looking for something valuable to pawn. Still, we don't see much crime in Blue Lake. Kinda took everybody by surprise. Congressman Tucker's in a downright uproar. But Mrs. Lipowitz is fine. As mouthy as a parrot and sharp as a bear claw, but apparently as clumsy as a fawn. She knocked her phone clear off the wall when trying to call 911."

"Huh, that's weird," I said, trying not to freak out. That noise I'd heard coming from her garage had probably been whoever was robbing her. I tried not to think about what might have happened had they seen me, and focused on Mrs. Lipowitz. "I've heard people don't know their own strength when adrenaline rushes through them. Did she say anything else?"

"Nope." He took a bite of his chicken, and I wilted with relief. "Except for one thing. Sherriff Hamilton and I chalked it up to the bump on her head. She kept going on and on about some superhero who saved her life. Called himself Harry Weird."

"Hard Wired," Mel and I chimed in simultaneously.

"Excuse me?" Coach looked at us both funny.

Mel and I locked eyes. "Uh, we heard the name was Hard Wired, not Harry Weird," I said. "Who would willingly call themselves Harry Weird?"

"Yeah, and who says the superhero is a boy?" Mel Asked, looking miffed. "Why can't a girl be a superhero?"

He blinked. "Guess I just assumed the superhero was a boy. Either way, can you imagine? A real live superhero in Blue Lake?"

"After that freaky kryptonite they found in the woods, I'd say anything's possible, even superheroes." Mel's mischievous eyes sparkled. "Personally, I think every superhero should have a fabulous sidekick."

I knew she hadn't forgotten the sidekick angle.

"Wonder if this Hard Wired is smart enough to find herself one," she went on. "They could even be best friends. Don't you think that would be cool?"

"I think you've been watching too much TV, right Sam?" Coach Stuart said.

"I think you're right, Coach." I glared at Mel. "I personally don't think superheroes exist."

"Only time will tell," Mrs. Stuart chimed in.

"I agree," I said. Mrs. Stuart couldn't be more right... only time would tell.

"I'll get it," I shouted to my mom--who was down the hall in the gym with her personal trainer--as I jogged to the foyer.

I opened the door, forgetting to look through the peephole as usual. We already had a top-of-the-line security system--the only one in Blue Lake--but that was my mom for you. I blinked as I focused on the gray-haired petite dynamo standing before me.

"Gram!" I threw myself into her arms, and she hugged me tight.

Gabriella Fontana-Granger was sixty and looked every inch of it, but she didn't care. Mom might be beautiful and Dad might be a slob, but Gram was smack dab in the middle like me. She was perfect in my eyes. She'd never cared for makeup or hair color, preferring to spend her time fighting for causes and standing up for things she believed in. That's why helping people was so important to me. It was a part of my DNA.

Gram had a heart of gold just like Dad and was generous to a fault, but she was not someone you wanted to cross. According to Dad, Mom had pretty much crossed her worse than anyone when she filed for divorce against Gram's only child--her baby boy.

"Samantha, dear, you're as lovely as ever. Let me have a look at you." Gram let go and stepped back to study me.

Just one more reason why I loved her to pieces. She tsked, grabbing her suitcase and pushing past me with a determined gait as she headed straight for the kitchen.

"You're too thin. You need to eat." She pulled out pots and pans, not even bothering to unpack. Did I mention my Gram is Italian? Dad is only half and I'm only a quarter, but Gram is full blown. Mom, on the other hand, is Irish. Yet another strike against her.

I giggled. "Gram, I'm not even close to being too thin, but I love you for saying so."

"Ah, so you don't want my special lasagna, then."

"I said I wasn't too thin. I never said I was stupid. My mouth is watering already." I slid on the barstool and leaned my elbows on the island as I watched her whip around the kitchen like a clock wound too tight. The kitchen my mom never used. Her five star chef did all the cooking, or we ordered take-out.

"So, Gram, why are you here?" I broke off a piece of Italian bread and sank my teeth in, the yeasty taste melting over my taste buds as I closed my eyes in heaven. She must have stopped by my favorite bakery on her way from the airport.

"Because you're here, and I go where you go." She nodded as though that were final, then continued layering her lasagna. She paused, her hands falling still. Gram's hands never fell still. She couldn't talk, think or even breathe without moving her hands, which meant something was seriously wrong.

"I'm worried about you." She pointed her wooden spoon at me.

Uh-oh. "Me?" I swallowed hard. "What did I do?" I squeaked.

"I don't know, what did you do?" Her gaze locked onto mine and wouldn't let go. "That's what I'm here to find out."

"I didn't do anything, I swear. Why would you think that?"

"Your guidance counselor, Mrs. Sweeny, called your parents. When your father told me, I headed straight to the airport."

"Oh." Well, what could I say to that? My shoulders slumped, and my appetite vanished.

"To say she was concerned would be putting it mildly. So I repeat, what did you do?"

How much did I tell Gram? She'd always been the one person I could confide in, with no fear of judgment. But with the question of my health on the line because of the freaky stuff inside me, would she freak out like I knew my parents would? I wasn't sure what to do. "I-I--"

"I'm starving. Must be Grandma Granger has arrived," my mother exclaimed as she breezed into the kitchen, freshly showered and dressed for work. She plastered on a stiff fake smile for my benefit, then said, "Too bad I won't be here for your delicious cooking, Gabby, but I have a business dinner. Some important complications have come to my attention that must be dealt with right away. You don't mind, do you?"

Gram's face remained smile free. "That's what I'm here for, Victoria. To spend time with my only grandchild, since her own mother's obviously too busy."

"Yes, well, we're lucky to have you." Mom ignored Gram's jab, kissed my cheek, and then left without another word.

Gram just grunted and slid the lasagna in the oven, then wiped her hands on her apron and turned to me, "Okay, Sammy, what have you gotten yourself into?"

"Nothing really. I've just been going though some weird stuff."

"What kind of weird stuff?"

I looked into eyes the same shade of brown as mine, and was tempted to tell her the whole story, but then the phone rang. "Shouldn't you get that? It might be important." I bit my lip and winced as I waited for her reaction.

She stood silent so long, I was afraid she was having a stroke. "Gram?"

"It's settled then. I'm going to extend my visit until I figure this out. I have a feeling you need some serious help, child."

"You have no idea," I muttered under my breath and groaned. Fooling Mom and dad was one thing.

Fooling Gram would take a miracle.

8

LOVE IS ON THE MENU

Monday afternoon I walked the halls of Blue Lake Junior High, my eyes darting left and right, searching the faces of all the students and faculty. I hoped no one could tell that on the outside I was dressed as Samantha Granger, but underneath my jeans and sweater lay my Super Flash costume. Like I said, the name was a work in progress. No way was I risking being called Harry Weird again.

It wasn't exactly cold enough for a sweater--64 degrees with 10 mph winds from the SSW, according to my internal Doppler radar--but I was petrified someone would see my sparkly chest through just a T-shirt.

Hearing voices down the hall, I looked up and saw a man with slicked back, dark brown hair and sunglasses. I'd seen him at the Salvation Army earlier this week, and was now talking to Principal Norton. I couldn't help wondering who he was and what he wanted.

"Oh, my God, Sam, I heard the news," Maria said, distracting me. Her heels clickety-clacked on the floor as she walked over to me and grabbed my arms, then yanked her hand back. "Ow, I broke a nail," she whined.

It was still a mystery how this girl could kick the crap out of a soccer ball without blinking but be a princess off the field. I peeked back down the hall, but Dark Shades Man was gone. Maybe I was just being paranoid.

Shrugging, I focused back on Maria and patted her arm. "I'll treat you to both a mani and a pedi if you'll tell me what you're talking about."

"Well--"

The bell rang, and I swore there was some kind of bell conspiracy going on. "Walk with me to lunch?" I steered her down another hallway. "Now, what were you saying?"

"Well, Ali was talking smack about that freaky Morse Code thing you did last week. I mean, like, let it go already, right? She's just jealous--"

"Maria."

"Fine, chill, girlfriend. You're so uptight. Don't worry, once your parents' divorce is final, you'll feel much better."

My stomach flipped at the word divorce. "I'm sorry, but I don't want to talk about that. Nothing personal, it's just a touchy subject for me."

"No problem. I can't blame you for not wanting to talk about your dad getting fired from Electro for doing something illegal."

"Excuse me?" My dad got demoted, not fired, and then he left. But since my parents never talk about what really happened, I couldn't say for sure he hadn't done anything illegal. Still, this was my dad they were talking about. I stared her down and ground my teeth.

She held up her hands. "Hey, relax. I'm just repeating what Ali said."

"Well, don't."

"Sorry, but it's all over school already."

I closed my eyes, inhaled deep, and relaxed my shoulders as I tried for a calm I didn't feel, striving to forget about things I had no control over. "Anyway," I finally said, "you know how it is when people talk about you. I just need to know what they're saying."

"You don't have to worry. Seriously. People think it's cool."

"What's cool?"

"You know, your photographic memory."

"Oh ... that." I laughed a little too loud.

"When Ali kept going on and on, trying to get stuff started, Mel cut her off and told Ali she didn't know what she was talking about. That your grandmother has a photographic memory, and something about a recessive gene being dormant inside you, but now it's awake. I'm not gonna lie, some people think you're weird, but I think you rock." Maria beamed, excitement vibrating from her every pore. "So tell me ... what am I thinking?"

"How should I know?"

Her face fell. "Mel's crazy. You don't have a photographic memory."

"Maria, I'd only know what you were thinking if I had ESP."

"Bummer. What's a photographic memory then?"

"It's when you see something and never forget it."

"Wow, that really is cool." She looked around as though we were on a top secret covert operation. "Can I tell people?"

"Sure. Tell the world." Hopefully, it would stop any crazy rumors from spreading, and no one would put me to the test. If they did, I'd just Google the information in my brain or download the operating manual.

Maria's stomach growled. "We'd better get to lunch before it's over. Do you want to put your bag in your locker?"

"No!"

Her eyes widened.

"It's that time of the month. I sort of need my 'supplies' if you know what I mean."

"Ah, gotcha." She winked. "I'm going to grab us a seat with the soccer team. Come over when you're done."

"I will." I took a breath as I headed for the lunch line, exhausted over trying to keep it all together. I was melting. With my luck, I probably smelled by now. I tried to discreetly tip my head to the side and sniff, but didn't smell anything. Thank God no one saw me. I didn't need to be any weirder.

———

"You smell great," a voice said from right behind my ear.

I whirled around, feeling the heat flood my face. "Trevor! How's it hangin'?" I winced. "I mean, what's up?"

"Nothing." He grabbed a tray and loaded it. "I've been grounded all weekend." A whiff of his cologne mixed with something distinctly Trevor filled my head and made me dizzy. He was the one who smelled great. "You coming?" He looked back at me just standing there.

I snatched a tray and filled it as we talked. "I heard your dad wasn't happy you skipped practice."

"I've had to do all kinds of extra work." Trevor's emerald green eyes locked onto mine. "Some things are worth the risk." My temperature rose even more. He frowned. "You okay? You look like you're going to pass out."

"I'm fine, just a little warm." I was more than fine. He

hadn't mentioned Ali even once. I looked at his firm lips, and my temperature climb yet another degree.

His gaze ran over me, lingering on my sweater. "It's going to be seventy today. Isn't that sweater wool?"

"Every last thread," I groaned. "In my defense, it was freezing this morning. Guess I should start watching the weather before school from now on."

"Don't you have anything on underneath?"

"You don't want to see what I have under this sweater." I scoffed.

His brows crept up, but he didn't say a word. His eyes didn't drop beneath my collarbone anymore, either.

"I, uh, mean I spilled orange juice on my T-shirt this morning before school and didn't have time to change."

His hand bumped mine, and a charge ran right through my glove and straight up my arm. I gulped, feeling my pulse kick up several notches.

He stared at me as though fascinated, like he didn't quite know what to do with me. I sighed, my internal thermostat skyrocketing like my X-Box after an all day Mario Cart marathon. If I didn't know better, I'd swear there was steam coming out of my ears--probably an internal smoke alarm.

I could feel the same pressure building within me, but then Trevor started talking to another kid in line ahead of us, and my body cooled. The boy behind me started to flirt, but I remained unaffected. Hmmm. Weird.

Mel came in and grabbed a carton of milk, gave me an 'ask him' look, then darted to the head of the line to pay the cashier.

What was I doing? Could I really ask Trevor out? No more incidents had happened all weekend. Maybe my brain rerouting itself and sending me to Old Lady Lipowitz rescue had been a fluke. A short circuit of sorts. In fact, no more incidents of any kind had happened. Maybe things were getting back to normal.

I inhaled sharply, then blurted, "What did you want to ask me at the game the other day?"

Trevor jerked in surprise, focusing on me once more. I could have sworn his face flushed a little, but then he recovered: calm, cool, and serious. "You mean the game where you ran away from me?"

"If I remember right, you had to leave, too." I paid the cashier, and we stepped out of the lunch line together and into the cafeteria.

The hum of conversation mixed with dishes and silver clanking and teachers scolding filled the air. We wove our way through the throng of students heading to their seats on the long benches. Pausing half way to our tables, we both searched for our friends. I usually sat with the soccer girls, and he with the football players. Gossip Queen Ali and the Burdick Twins sat somewhere in between, and Simon usually sat by himself with his nose in a book.

Ali's jaw dropped open, and she glared at me before plastering on a bored expression. I ignored her, and smiled a smile that said everything I wanted to tell her.

"Yo, Trevor, hurry up man. I want some of your fries," Scott Randolph hollered above the noise.

Scott was the kicker for the football team. A tall and skinny former soccer player. Mel had known him since they played together in their younger coed soccer days, but he'd done the unthinkable: Switched over to the dark side to play football.

I knew Mel and Scott had a unique bond throughout the years, teasing each other relentlessly, but defending each other to the end. He'd pummel anyone who made fun of her crooked teeth, and she'd throttle anyone who said a word about his big nose. It was only recently that <u>she'd</u> done the unthinkable ... started crushing on him.

"All the fries in the world won't improve your punting, there, slick," Melody said. "When you going to let me show you how it's done?"

"When you grow a few inches, shrimp," Scott countered back, grinning wide. Scott's lanky frame to Mel's curvy short one should make them look ridiculous together, but it didn't. Somehow, they just fit.

Melody grinned wider. "You don't need long legs to kick a ball, meathead. You need skill. I have plenty." She looked at me, but I shook my head, and she frowned.

If she kept things business as usual, Scott would never notice her in a different way. She needed to surprise him. Then again, who was I to say anything? I talked like a bumbling idiot when Trevor was around.

"Tell it to someone who cares." Scott elbowed a fellow teammate and laughed.

"Duh, like I would ever care about you?" Mel elbowed Maria, mimicking Scott in an exaggerated way while trying to look like she lacked a few brain cells.

Scott's face hardened, the teasing smile gone. Mel didn't look any happier.

Trevor shook his head. "Rain check on the conversation?"

"You mean a rain check on the rain check since that's what you said last time." I smirked.

"Something like that." One side of Trevor's mouth hitched up in a rare lopsided grin. "I'm holding you to it this time. No more disappearing acts."

"What can I say? It takes a special guy to pin me down." I couldn't believe the stuff that was coming out of my mouth.

Maybe Super Flash was giving me a newfound confidence. Whatever it was, I liked it … and it was working.

His eyes glittered. "I'm pretty good at tackling."

"And I'm suddenly great at blocking."

He smiled fully for the first time since I'd met him. "Game on."

"Good." I glanced at Mel. She was obviously still mad at Scott, what he said actually hurt her. I took a deep breath and did a little something unthinkable myself. "Because there's something I need to ask you, too."

9

DOUBLE TROUBLE

Later that night I slipped into the back row of the amphitheater at Blue Lake University, waiting for the seminar on electromagnetic fields to begin. I'd seen the advertisement while researching what might have happened to me, and thought it sounded like a starting point. The place was packed with college students and scientists and.... I slid down in my seat.

What was Simon doing here?

He sat a couple rows down from the special team of scientists. They'd set up shop right here at Blue Lake University, taking over one of the labs. Everything they were doing was supposed to be top secret. They didn't plan to share their results until they finished their studies. The place was secured tighter than Mom's bank account these days. She and Gram were butting heads, and whatever was going on at Electro Corp had Mom stressed out more than usual.

Some physicist started talking, and my ears perked up. He went on about a lot of things I didn't understand, but then he said something that had me sitting up straight and listening closer. He spoke about the phenomenon behind energy being absorbed when two highly charged bodies collide. Like when stars in space collide, the electromagnetic field of one body is absorbed into the other.

I sucked in a breath. Oh my God, that must be what happened when to me while holding my Electro Wave. Things couldn't get any more "highly charged." I happened to be the least charged of the three, absorbing both the Electro Wave and the power of the crystal.

I still didn't understand how it all worked, I just knew without a shadow of a doubt that something incredible had happened to me. I glanced at Simon who scribbled notes furiously in a small notebook. I bet if anyone could help me figure it all out, he could. I just had to find the right time and place to talk to him.

Scanning the room full of strange faces, I decided now was <u>not</u> the time. My hand vibrated, and I jumped. I didn't think I'd ever get used to that feeling. I jogged out of the auditorium, colliding with someone. "Whoops, sorry," I said, glancing up. My eyes sprang wide.

Dark Shades Man steadied my arm and slipped off his glasses all in one smooth motion. "Ma'am," was all he said, barely glancing at me as he made his way into the room, his gaze moving continuously.

I frowned, but then my hand vibrated again, so I jerked myself into motion once more and took off down the hall. I rounded a corner and sat in a private nook, then pulled off my glove. Sighing over the Caller ID, I tapped the send button with my fingertip to answer the call.

"Oh, hi, Mel. It's just you."

"Don't sound so excited."

"I am. I just thought maybe it would be Trevor."

"Still no word?"

"Nope. Guess you were wrong--oh, hang on a sec, I have a text coming in." I snapped my fingers to click on the text so I could view the blue-green veiny message.

Trevor!

Trevor: Hey. Going to the game tonight?
  Me: What game?
(Translation: Like everyone didn't know.)
  Trevor: The ONLY game. Friday night lights!
  Me: Not sure. I might have other plans with Mel. (Translation: Like we wouldn't change them in a nanosecond!)
  Trevor: Bring her. Scott was asking about her. Maybe we can have that rain check convo after.
  Me: Maybe.
(Translation: absolutely!)
  Trevor: Gotta run.
  Me: Later.

I snap-clicked back over, knowing Mel still hung on the line.

"Well?" she blurted. "Who was it?"

I laughed. "Looks like you got your double date. Sort of."

"Get home," she said after she finished shrieking. "I'll be right over."

I grinned wide. Progress ... on all fronts.

Later that night we sat in the bleachers of Blue Lake Junior High, watching our team kick Snow Ridge Junior

High's butt, big-time. "There's something so cute about a boy in a football uniform." I purred.

"Cuz it makes them look like seniors with all those pads emphasizing what their mamas gave them. Yum yum." Mel giggled, shivering as the chilly October wind picked up.

I squirmed, trying not to scratch, sweating my butt off. "I'm sick of wearing this costume every day. Thank God my mom doesn't do the laundry. I have to wash it constantly. It's starting to get worn out."

"Maybe you don't need a costume anymore. Nothing has happened for a week. Maybe your little problem has gone away."

"Somehow I doubt I'd be that lucky."

"Only one way to find out."

"What do you mean?" I looked to the side to see her face.

"How wide is Buford's butt in those pads?"

My head whipped straight, then my left eye zoomed in and focused on Buford--aka our two-hundred-pound lineman--and the right eye snapped a picture of his butt. My corpus collosum allowed the information in the right hemisphere of my brain to shoot to the left hemisphere for calculation. Once the answer was determined, my brain stem coordinated the message and then my motor neurons carried that information to my vocal chords.

I spit out the results robotically in every measurement known to man and three languages to boot.

"Thanks, Mel. That's an image that will be tattooed forever on my brain ... literally. Why couldn't you have asked the same question about Trevor?" I groaned as the game ended, and the players jogged off the field to the locker room. My eyes had crossed after that image.

A shower of hot liquid covered the front of my shirt. I gasped, surging to my feet, and coming face to face with Ali.

She covered her mouth with her hand. "Oh my gosh, did I do that? I'm so sorry." Her eyes twinkled.

"You did that on purpose," Mel snapped, searching her pockets.

"Here," Simon said, jumping to his feet from a couple rows behind us and shoving a stack of napkins at Mel.

Mel reluctantly took the napkins and handed them to me.

"Thanks, Simon," I said wiping my face.

Ali ignored Mel, staring me down and feigning horror. "Better go change before that sweater gets ruined." Burdick One and Burdick Two chuckled and snorted like hyenas beside her. "Or you can find one of mine at your favorite store. You know, the Salvation Army." She paused, and half the stadium stopped to gawk at us.

Everyone started eyeing my clothes, and my face flamed red. "I help out; I don't shop there." Well, not entirely true, but no one needed to know about my superhero costume.

"Silly me, my mistake. Speaking of helping out, I've got to go. Daddy has another community service job for Trevor." Ali sashayed over to the gym doors.

I squinted, positive I saw Dark Shades Man in the crowd of spectators. After rubbing my eyes, I looked again. No one was there. I must be losing my mind.

"One of these days she's going to get what's coming to her." Mel grabbed more napkins and poured bottled water over them, dabbing at my shirt. "Back to what we were talking about. Your problems might not have gone away, but you only need a costume when you get called to the rescue. That has only happened once. Maybe you won't get rerouted again."

"I'm not taking any chances. I hope Trevor doesn't notice how messy I look."

She tapped my arm and pointed behind me. "You're about to find out."

"But Ali--"

"Is a pea brain. Forget about her. Here they come. Let's start walking. Act natural." Mel jumped up and led the way.

The stadium emptied as the players headed off the field. Ali intercepted Trevor, smiled coyly up at him as she said something. He glanced my way, cut her off short, then headed into the locker room. Ali stood there, stunned. After a moment, she stomped off to the parking lot. Score one for me. I smiled on the inside as we sat there forever waiting for Trevor and Scott to come out of the locker room.

When we finally saw them walk out the door, we turned toward the parking lot, trying not to look too obvious. They caught up, and we all walked together with Mel and Scott behind Trevor and me.

"You made it." Trevor smiled just a little, his hair still damp from his shower, the strands curling at the bottom. "I'm glad."

"Me too." I tore my eyes away so he wouldn't catch me staring.

"Rough day?" He glanced at the hot chocolate stains on my sweater.

"I think I can fix the damage. I might have lost the battle, but this opponent wasn't that hot. Mostly full of steam."

"That's good."

There was a pause in our conversation, so I jumped to fill it. "You guys played a great game."

"See, now that's how you handle a ball." Scott scrubbed a hand over his flat-top while grinning at Mel as they drew up beside us.

"Puh-lease. You wouldn't last five minutes around me if

you had to handle a <u>real</u> ball." Mel snorted, flipping her long curls over her shoulder.

"Right, like a soccer ball is a real ball." Scott poked her in the side.

"It's better than a stupid football." She poked him back.

"Lucky for you, I've got one in my bag."

"Get out!" Mel shoved him in the chest. "Scott Randolph has a soccer ball? Why? You switching back to a <u>real</u> sport?"

"In your dreams."

"How'd you guess?" Mel lowered her voice, her cheeks flaming red, but she never broke eye contact.

I held my breath, wanting to hug her for her bravery.

"I borrowed my sister's just in case I ran into you tonight," Scott responded, searching her face with intense eyes.

"You're the one who probably dreams about me." She threw back at him, seeming to grow more comfortable with her new plan of attack.

Scott's grin reached all the way across his face. "How'd you guess?" he matched her word for word. "I'm still better than you, shrimp."

"Prove it. Race ya." Mel took off, leaving Scott surprised and grinning, but not for long.

"Cheater," he yelled after her, then bolted at a full sprint to catch up to her.

"Now that we're finally alone," Trevor said, slowing his pace and slipping my gloved hand into his, "there's something I've been trying to ask you for a while now."

Please don't let my hand vibrate, I mentally begged, and there went that ping-ponging heart as my system overheated once more. Why did my body react this way every time Trevor got too close? It didn't happen around other boys. The same pressure as before built within me. I could feel my skin tingle and my limbs quake as my forehead and upper lip beaded up.

He searched my face. "You okay? You're starting to sweat."

"I'm fine. I'm just a sweater." A sweater? He was going to think I was gross. "Uh, I mean, I don't smell or anything, I just sweat when I get nervous. Not that you make me nervous, just this ... this ... Look, a shooting star." I yanked my hand from his and pointed to the cloud covered sky. You couldn't see a star if you tried. "Make a wish," I said on a giggle, sounding on the verge of hysteria.

His eyes never left my face. "I wish you'd relax around me." He bumped my shoulder with his.

Relax? Impossible. My body sizzled, and I felt faint. I struggled to focus as his face began to blur before me. Then I swayed. If I fainted, there'd be no consoling me.

"Whoa, hey, take it easy." He reached out to steady me with both hands, and somehow I ended up in his arms. Bubble, bubble, bubble went the pressure cooker within me.

"I just feel, sort of, dizzy," I rasped. I wrapped my arms around him, and he tightened his hold until we were in a full embrace, our faces only inches apart.

His eyes traced every speck of my face, the strands of his hair tickling my chin. His green eyes were so deep and sparkled like nothing I'd ever seen. He was gorgeous, but the last thing I wanted was for another person I cared about to let me down.

I stared at him long and hard, then finally said, "I don't want to get hurt."

He stared back just as long and hard, then answered, "I would never hurt you."

He straightened my crooked glasses and then, as if in

slow motion, he bent his head bent down toward mine. I sucked in a sharp breath. This was it. The moment I'd been dreaming of. I felt my eyelids flutter closed and could feel his breath on my face when. . . a sharp pain seared my brain.

"Ow!" I screamed and grabbed my head as a bright white light followed by a phone number flashed before my eyes. "No!" My body jerked out of Trevor's grasp, and I felt cold for the first time that night as I headed for the road.

"What'd I do?" Trevor asked, looking confused.

I knew exactly how he felt. I couldn't believe this was happening to me again. Now, of all times--the exact moment when Trevor was about to kiss me! It was so unfair. "You didn't do anything," I said, not having a clue how to explain what was happening. I shivered, unable to shake the chills. My limbs felt weak, yet my legs continued to move.

"Then what's the problem?" He walked along beside me. At least by this time, I'd figure out how to balance. No more victory dances.

"I forgot. Gram is supposed to pick me up after the game. Mom's been so busy lately. If Gram doesn't get me home on time, Mom will call your dad and we'll both be in trouble."

"Can't you call her?" He put his hand on my arm to try to stop me, but I just kept walking.

"I'm grounded from using my cell phone." I shrugged and looked away, hoping he'd stop asking me so many questions.

"That sucks." He caught back up to me.

"I've found ways around it. Whoa!" I said as my body made a sharp left turn, catching me off balance. "New shoes," I said by way of explanation.

"Now where are you going?" Trevor asked, throwing his hands up in the air and changing directions.

If this was what it was like to get old and lose control of your body, I'd never look forward to another birthday. I'd give anything for someone to put me out of my misery right now. "I know a short cut."

"Through the woods?" he asked. "Where's your Gram picking you up?"

"Sam, where are you going? I thought my dad was giving you a ride home?" Mel shouted from Scott's side.

"Change of plans, remember, sidekick?" I gave her a knowing look.

Awareness dawned on her face. "That's right." Mel jogged over and blocked Trevor's path. "You're riding home with Scott, right?"

"Right," he said in a distracted voice as he tried to look around her. I couldn't even enjoy that he wanted to be with me. He almost kissed me ... and I missed it.

"Think they would give me a ride down to the pizza shop on the corner? That's where my dad is picking me up." She lowered her voice shyly. "I want to spend more time with Scott."

"I guess." Trevor gave me one last concerned look as I disappeared into the woods, but I heard him say, "It's getting dark. Aren't you worried she's going to get lost? She looks like she's ready to pass out."

Mel snorted. "A couple weeks ago, for sure. But since she has her Gram's photographic memory, not so much. Don't worry about her, she'll be fine."

"Whatever." He walked away, his wall firmly back in place.

I wasn't so sure Mel was right. I truly did feel like I could pass out at any moment, and I wasn't any happier about leaving Trevor than he was. I didn't want any part of this whole superhero thing. I needed to talk to Simon, and soon.

There had to be a way to reverse what had happened.

I ground my teeth as I stripped off my glasses and clothes along the way and stuffed them in my bag, and then pulled on my boots and mask while fighting my constantly moving legs. Not easy by any means, but it worked. With my hair pulled out of its ponytail, glasses gone, and half my face covered, no one would be able to tell who I was.

I stashed my bag in the woods behind the school and let my feet lead the way. I trudged through the woods for what seemed like forever. Finally, I broke through a clearing and gaped.

Blue Lake University? The same university where the special team of scientists had set up a lab to study the crystal. I had a bad feeling things were about to get more complicated.

10

BATTERIES NOT INCLUDED

What if those science guys spotted me? With my heart pounding, I let my feet led the way to the back entrance of Salmon Run Hall. My legs kept moving forward until I bumped into the door, but it was locked.

A guy opened it from inside. "Kicking it won't help, dude. You need a key." He looked me over, then finally let me in. "Uh, interesting, costume."

"Thanks," I said. Why did everyone assume this superhero was a boy?

"Isn't Halloween like a week away still?"

"Just taking it for a test run ... dude." I slipped into the empty stairwell and climbed to the top floor, my legs burning all the way. If these rescues kept up, I'd be in great shape in no time.

I came to a stop outside a dorm room, and regained control of my body. The halls were empty. This didn't make any sense. I just wanted to go home. I turned around and took a step, then stopped. Helping people was what I'd done my whole life. As much as I didn't want to be here, I couldn't walk away. Gram's voice in my head would never allow it. I knocked, but no one answered. Whoever had called 911 was hurt, incapacitated, possibly dying inside this room.

"Don't worry, I'll save you," I said, feeling a little weird, but knowing I had to do something. I shoved hard at the door with my shoulder, and it opened, propelling me inside ... right on top of a young frat boy, based on the Greek letters displayed on his hat.

"Dude, get off me," he croaked.

"Right, um, tell me where it hurts, I guess, and I'll try to help." I scrambled off him and sat on my knees careful not to touch anything. The room looked as though a bomb had gone off.

He grabbed his chest, distracting me. "Right here."

"Oh my God, you're having a heart attack." I was about to download a video on how to give CPR when a strong whiff of liquor made my eyes cross. My jaw fell open, and I stared at the guy closely. "Why exactly did you call 911?"

"I've been robbed," he slurred. "My ex-girlfriend stole my sense of humor." He started laughing.

"You're not dying, you're drunk," I snapped. Real people were getting robbed, and this guy had the nerve to mess around.

Unbelievable.

"I'm a loser. Sitting home alone on a Friday, feeling sorry for myself." He opened his eyes and grinned. "Hey, did Rooster send you here to keep an eye on me? You're kind of young--your voice hasn't even changed yet." He focused on my outfit and squinted. "What's your name?"

"Super Flash."

"Supper Flask?"

"It's Super Flash," I ground out, knowing I'd once again have to change my superhero name.

"Why are you here?"

"To help you." Unfortunately.

"Hey, wait a minute. You must be that superhero everyone's been talking about. I thought your name was Harry Weird?"

"Long story." I inhaled slowly and counted to ten. "Now, help me before you pass out." He wrapped his arms around me, and I struggled to lift him toward the couch. He fell on top of me, and I sank into the cushions. I'd need two showers after this.

"I wasn't even supposed to be here, you know. My roommate is kind of uptight. He has this big test he's studying for," Frat Boy mumbled. "He was furious when I came back, so he took off. Now I'm the loser sitting home on a Friday night with a stinking kid for a baby sitter." He fell off the couch. "Hey, where you going?"

"You need a lot more than my help, pal." I tried to open his dorm room door, but it was stuck--like something was wedged against it from the outside. Fire alarms wailed throughout the building, and I smelled smoke. "Oh my God, the building is on fire, and someone blocked the door."

"Guess I'm not the only one who doesn't like my roommate," Frat Boy said and crawled toward the window.

"Help," I screamed over and over, but no one answered. Sirens screeched off in the distance, and panic set in. I could not get caught, or everyone would know my true identity. "Think, Sam, think," I muttered as I paced.

"Who's Sam?" Frat Boy asked as he tugged on the window to no avail.

"I said Spam. Eat Spam."

"Huh?"

"Nevermind."

Why was this happening to me? There was no way I could physically carry him or help him down a fire ladder without us both falling. I searched the room for something, anything, and then I noticed rock climbing gear in the corner. I read the nameplate on the equipment bag. Nelson Carmichael. Must be the roommate. Frat Boy was going to kill me for this one, but I couldn't think of anything else that would work.

Concentrating, I tapped into the internet and downloaded the instructions for propelling down the side of a building, the information burning a path through my brain. It zipped back and forth between my sensory and motor neurons like a neurological relay race, until finally rocketing down my spine and shooting the message to my limbs. My fingernails glowed blue-green and tingled with readiness.

I yelped, then swallowed my fear. No time for freaking out. I Googled the exact pressure point to hit on a double paned window so it would shatter, providing my cerebrum with the information I needed to escape this inferno.

I shoved Frat Boy out of the way, my glowing fingertips snatching a desk chair with a will of their own and smashing the window. With lightning speed, I rigged him to the rock climbing gear, stood him up, and faced him in front of the window.

"Hey, wait a minute, what are you doing? Sorry for whatever I did, dude."

"I'm the one who's sorry, and stop calling me dude." I winced and pushed hard. "I really am so sorry," I yelled as he tumbled out, wearing a shocked expression.

He screamed as he fell three stories, then grunted when the rope snapped tight. Crossing my burning fingers that had at least stopped glowing, I peeked outside and let out an explosion of air. The rope held. Exhausted and slightly dizzy, I quickly unrolled the fire ladder and scrambled down the side of the building as best I could past a dazed and smelly Frat Boy. Plugging my nose, I made my escape seconds before the fire department arrived.

Oh, yeah, he was definitely <u>not</u> going to be happy when he realized the little "accident" he'd had on the way down. I couldn't worry about that right now. There was something much bigger to worry about.

Like why someone had barred his dorm room door.

"HUH, THAT'S INTERESTING," DAD SAID FROM THE LIVING room of the apartment he'd rented in town. Simple and affordable with no sense of style whatsoever. It suited him perfectly.

He'd arrived at the same time as Gram, they just hadn't told me. They'd said they didn't want to overwhelm me, so they waited until he'd moved into his new place to spring the news. I still wasn't sure why he was here, exactly. He said it was only temporary; to help me settle in, given my odd behavior lately.

My gut told me something wasn't right.

"What's interesting, your job? You didn't get fired, did you? Because, you know, it's okay. You can tell me. I can handle it, really. I mean, you're back working for Electro, right?"

"Not exactly. It's complicated. You wouldn't understand." He glanced at me quick, then back to the TV. "But don't worry. I didn't get fired. I was referring to the news."

Congressman Tucker was talking about the rise in crime

in that smooth cultured voice of his and repeating his favorite phrase: "This ends now!"

"Oh, okay," I said, tuning out the TV and focusing on what mattered. I didn't care why Dad was here, I was just glad he'd come. Maybe now we would feel more like a family. I worried about who was going to take care of him when he was so far away.

I frowned, remembering mom's reaction to him showing up. When Electro transferred her here from San Jose, she chose a five-thousand-square-foot ultra modern contemporary house in the suburbs as her rental, trying to make my life feel less like a rental. Dad came back and rented a fixer-upper apartment just off Main Street. He said it had charm, just like him. Mom agreed it was just like him ... a complete and utter mess. Still, I refused to lose hope of them reconciling.

"What's interesting?" Gram asked from her usual spot in the kitchen, staying true to her word about going wherever I did. Since Dad arrived, that meant rotating weeks in and out of town.

I sat at the dining room table doing my homework and tried to tune them out. Pretty hard without my iPod, but for once, Mom was right. Dad had agreed on no more gadgets. They just didn't realize I could download a whole playlist inside my head. I started singing out loud by accident.

Dad narrowed his eyes at me.

"No iPod, see." I held up my hands. "I'm just singing to the songs in my head."

Gram gave me a look that said I'm not going to rest until I figure out what you're up to.

Dad grunted. "They just said something about a super-hero that goes by the name Supper Flask. Doesn't sound very heroic to me. I'm telling you, there's more than one kid involved here."

I choked, spraying soda all over the table as it shot out my nose. "What did you say?" I sputtered, putting my mental iPod on pause. I was glued to their every word now.

"Oh, Sammy, look at the mess you made. You should be drinking milk. That stuff is going to rot your insides. Go and get cleaned up." Gram bustled over to wipe off my homework before it was ineligible.

"In a sec. I'm curious to hear more about this latest superhero. Aren't you?" I met her eyes.

She stared at me for a full minute, then finally said, "Oh, that superhero."

"You mean you heard about it, too?" Dad asked.

"I heard about it earlier at the grocery store," Gram clarified. "You know how gossip flies in a small town. What did the news say?"

"Apparently some college guy got drunk and called 911, but the call never went through. This superhero showed up instead. That fire was set deliberately, and a chair was wedged against the boy's door. Makes you wonder if this kid set the fire so he could look like a superhero."

"She," I corrected.

"She?" Dad and Gram said simultaneously.

I looked up and saw them staring at me funny. "I just mean, you never know. You know?" Sheesh! I might not want to be a superhero, but no one seemed to think a girl could pull off the job. What was wrong with everyone?

Dad shrugged. "The point is that boy could have been seriously hurt."

"Oh my," Gram said.

"Huh," I scoffed. "Super Flash could have gotten hurt in

the fire, too, you know. Did the news say anything else about this superhero?" I asked.

"Just that the police think he," he glanced at me and winked, "or she, is some kid looking for attention. They think the culprit might be one of the kids behind the recent string of robberies and break-ins, and now this fire."

"That's crazy. From what I've heard, all she's done is help people," I said.

"Do you know this kid?" Dad looked at me curiously.

"It's not right, that's all." I stared down at my homework and started working again so he'd stop asking me questions.

"You might be right, but even Congressman Tucker has his suspicions about this superhero or heroes. The paper said he's offered a reward for the unveiling of any one of them, vowing to make lowering the recent increase in crime in Blue Lake the focus of his campaign."

"From what I've seen, that man will do anything to be in the spotlight. His daughter's just like him," I added. At least having my dad show up had put an end to her nasty rumor about him being arrested. Although, I still didn't know the details, and I had a feeling Ali wasn't done with me yet.

"Well, he'll certainly get his chance. Blue Lake is crawling with media." Dad shook his head. "All because of this bizarre thing that fell from the sky."

"Forget the crystal. Who wants some crazy kid on the loose, pretending to be a superhero of all things?" Gram waved her hands in the air.

I gaped at her. "Gram, I'm sure she's not all that bad. She was probably just trying to help."

"Which she has no business doing, if you ask me." She pointed her finger at me. "She should let the trained professionals do their job."

"Maybe she can't help herself. Did you ever think of that?"

"Well, that could be a problem then." Her eyes met mine and held. "Maybe she needs to work harder to control her impulses."

"I'm sure she's trying. Maybe it's not that easy."

"The special team of scientists who are studying that unidentified foreign object aren't so sure this superhero is harmless," Dad chimed in, listening carefully to the news and looking pensive. "They think the kid might be linked to the crystal falling from the sky since the incidents happened only a week apart. It does make you wonder how she knew the boy needed help if the call never went through."

Dad rubbed his stubbled cheeks, looking messier than usual. He'd been helping out in the Blue Lake offices while he was here. Whatever was happening at work was bothering him as much as Mom it seemed. "And what about Old Lady Lipowitz? She said the kid who rescued her went by the name Harry Weird. There's definitely something strange going on, that's for sure."

"You can say that again," Gram muttered.

"Mom, keep an eye on Sam? I need to go into work for a while. There's something I need to check. I'll take you to the farmer's market when I get back, okay?"

"Don't you worry about me." Her eyes drifted to mine and locked. "I'm not going anywhere."

"Not that I don't love having Gram here, Dad, but I'm thirteen, not three. I can watch myself."

"Said the girl who got lost in the woods and now can't find her very expensive cell phone. Gram stays, princess."

"Fine. I've got a headache," I said. "I'm going to lie down until Mel and Maria get here." I gathered my books and headed to my room, worrying about a whole new set of problems.

Like Ali's big-shot father offering a reward for Super Flash's identity. What if the scientists took matters into their own hands and tried to find the superhero themselves? They'd turn me into a lab experiment and dissect me. I had to find the reason I was being rerouted to help rescue the people whose 911 calls were mysteriously being blocked.

Then maybe, just maybe, I could get my alter ego to behave.

11

IT'S A DATE!

Later that day, Mel, Maria and I walked the mall, trying to figure out what we wanted to do next.

"Grab a slushy?" Mel asked.

"Sure," I said.

"Oh, and then we can get a mani and a pedi." Maria squealed. "You still owe me, Samantha."

Mel and I exchanged quick glances, and I made a fist with my gloved hand. "A pedi sounds awesome, but no mani for me. I'm not going to do anything to jinx the way I've been playing on goal."

I was getting better at coming up with believable excuses for all my strange behavior, but I longed for my old life. "You're too funny, Sam. And you think I'm weird."

We headed down the mall to the food court and sat at a small table in front of Slushyville.

"So, have you heard from Trevor since Friday night?" Mel asked me.

"Ohhh, dish. What happened Friday night?" Maria asked.

"Nothing. We just talked after the game, but then we got

interrupted and I had to go. I think he would have texted me by now if he liked me as anything more than a friend."

"You never know. Maybe he'll show up at the mall today," Mel said.

"You better not have told him to."

"I didn't. I told Scott." She actually blushed. Mel never blushed.

"Holy cow, guys. What did I miss? I knew I should have gone to the game. Are you guys going out, or what?"

"Nothing official ... yet." Mel giggled. "But he did end up walking me to the door of the pizza shop when they dropped me off, and he held my hand."

"Get out! That's awesome," I said. "I'm so happy for you."

"This could be you, too," she hinted. "Scott said Trevor really likes you, but you always disappear on him."

"Some things can't be helped." I glanced at Maria. I'd love to be in Mel's shoes right now, but that would never happen if I didn't get "Gamma Girl"--my latest moniker--under control.

"Hey, aren't those the science guys they showed on TV?" Maria asked.

I whipped around in my seat and spit my slushy all over the table. I really had to stop doing that.

"Ew, Sam. You got raspberry syrup all over my new blouse." Maria grabbed a napkin and headed off to the bathroom to put water on it. "This is dry clean only."

"Sorry," I hollered after her, then turned to Mel. "What are they doing here?"

"Don't panic," she said. "It's a Saturday, and we are at the mall. They could just be shopping?"

"They don't look like 'mall' type people." I locked eyes with one of the scientists, and started to jump up, but Mel grabbed my wrist.

"Calm down, Sam. The last thing you want to do is draw attention to yourself. It's not like they have x-ray vision and can see through your clothes or anything. No one but me knows what you're wearing underneath."

"Maybe they do have x-ray vision. You said yourself that the crystal could be kryptonite. What if the scientists aren't really scientists? They could be from outer space too," I pointed out in a near panic. "No wonder I can't find any research on the internet. Nothing like that crystal exists, and they know it."

"You're talking crazy now. Even if I do think the krypto is from space, I <u>don't</u> think the scientists are aliens. They're just running tests to make sure we are all safe. You know, not contaminated or anything."

"<u>We</u> aren't anything. <u>I</u> am the only one who was affected by that thing. I'm probably dying. If they catch me, they'll put me in quarantine for sure. Trevor thinks I disappear on him now? Ha!"

"Look, they're headed into the computer store, so obviously they're not 'onto' you. I'm sure you're not dying, but you just might have a heart attack if you don't stop freaking out.

"I can't help it." I took a few deep breaths. "Okay, I'm better now."

Moments later the science guys came back out, and another one made eye contact with me. My pulse tripped into overdrive, blood rushing through my veins, and I literally felt faint. Warning bells blared in my inner ear, beating a red alert message loud and clear on my ear drums, and suddenly several store alarms went off. Store clerks ran after the frowning scientists to check their pockets, then the scientists left the mall.

"Wow, that was weird," Mel said.

"Yeah, weird." I sat back in a daze, briefly wondering if I'd had anything to do with that. What more could possibly happen to me? I was too afraid to find out. I practiced more deep breathing and calmed my nerves, then looked over by the door and surged upright once more.

"Oh, my God, it's him again."

"HIM WHO?" MARIA ASKED AS SHE EMERGED FROM THE restroom.

"Uh, no one." I stared at Dark Shades Man. First the science guys, and now him. I had a feeling everyone was looking for Gamma Girl because of the award Ali's father's posted. I sank lower in my chair, feeling sick.

Dark Shades Man sat at an empty table in the far corner, watching everyone. A man in an overcoat and hat came in, spotted Dark Shades Man and jerked his head for the man to leave with him. Just before they reached the door, the newcomer collided with a group of teens, his hat tumbling to the floor. He turned around and swiped it up, giving me a glimpse of his face before he disappeared outside.

Dad?

"Oh, look who just came in," Mel said. "Know-it-all-Ali and her loyal dingledorfs--I mean, disciples--the Burdick Bozos."

I half heard what Mel said, still dazed and confused about why Dad was meeting with Dark Shades Man. What if Dad really had done something illegal? The way my life was going, anything was possible. I swallowed hard, hearing Gram in my head reminding me not to think the worst when I didn't know the facts.

I vowed to find out the truth one way or another.

"Well if it isn't Granola, I mean Granger. I don't know why I keep messing up your name," Ali said as she reached our table, looking picture perfect in every way, same as always. "My dad and I saw your mom earlier. She was with some bigwig Electro guy he knows. She didn't look so good. Like maybe she was nervous about something."

"Maybe something made her sick," I said. <u>Or someone</u>. I gave a casual shrug, then sipped my slushy, refusing to let her gossip get to me. I was relieved no one else had seen my dad talking to that mysterious guy.

"Oh, well, I hope she's okay." Ali looked down her long, aristocratic nose. "It would be a shame if she couldn't do her job and you had to move again."

Mel started to stand, but Maria grabbed her arm. "Sam's mom is tough. I'm sure she'll get over whatever is bothering her."

"You're bothering me," Burdick One chimed in, stepping up to Ali's side.

"What he said," Burdick Two added, stepping up to her other side.

"Back off, boys, you're crowding me." Ali rolled her eyes dramatically and pasted on her plastic smile. "What am I going to do with them?" She put her hand on her chest. "They're just so protective of me." Her eyes grew calculating. "Speaking of protective, did you hear the latest?"

We didn't say a word.

She went on anyway. "When I get the scoop on who the sleaze hiding behind this ridiculous superhero costume is, I'll ruin her. No way is it a gang of boys. It has to be a girl. No boy would be smart enough to pull off something like that."

We still didn't respond.

She set her jaw. "That was my cousin's boyfriend she practically killed on campus. No one messes with me or my family." Ali scanned the food court. She saw Trevor and Scott walk in, and her tone and mood changed instantly. "Well, gotto go--so much to do today. Toodles."

"I'll bet that superhero is shaking in her super-duper boots," Mel called after her.

Ali ignored her as she pranced over to Scott and Trevor. Both boys sat down to talk to her, causing Mel to turn her back on them and glare into her slushy.

"I hate to admit it, but if I were this superhero, I'd be a little nervous," Maria said. "We all love to secretly hate Ali, but none of us can deny she always gets the scoop."

That's exactly what I was afraid of.

"Hey, Mel," Simon walked up to our table.

Mel pushed her drink away. "Hi, Simon." She sighed.

He blinked, his face blushing all the way to his mangy mop of red hair. "See you in school on Monday."

She didn't answer, and he sauntered away.

"You're so mean to him." Maria frowned.

"I can't help it, he drives me nuts. He wears the same flannel shirts and jeans all the time. His hair hasn't been cut since the fifth grade. And, hello, the dude has never heard of a shower. It's like he's too busy being a computer geek to remember."

"He's not that bad," Maria said, staring after him with a thoughtful expression on her face. "Have you ever actually looked at him closely? He has perfect teeth and unusual colored eyes, kind of tawny like a lion's."

We both gaped at her. Was she for real?

"I'm just saying he could be decent looking if he cleaned himself up a little. It's just a shame, is all."

"Maria, you could have any guy you want. You are seriously not that desperate for a boyfriend." Mel grimaced.

"You just don't see his potential like I do. Besides, we live in Blue Lake. There aren't that many guys to choose from. And, most are just really into themselves."

"Let's hope not <u>all</u> are, because here come a few now." I swallowed hard as Trevor, Scott and half the football team made their way over to our table, leaving Ali and the Burdick Bozos to fend for themselves.

That alone was enough to make me adore him. Ali fumed and stalked out, with Dumb and Dumber hot on her heels.

"Hey, guys, what's up?" Maria asked, flipping her hair in a way she'd perfected years ago.

"Just a little something we like to call a par-tay down at the dead end of the OC road that borders farmer Johnson's property. We're having a Halloween party with a bonfire, food, and ... well, food, man. Wanna come?" Big Matt, the Fullback, asked Maria. "You can even dress up if you want."

"I guess I could." She gave a sigh. "That is, if my girls are game." She looked at Mel and me.

"I think I could handle a party," Mel glanced at Scott, "if it's not too lame." Her tone was bursting with irritation over his talking to Ali.

"Just be there at six. I'll show you lame." His pleasure at seeing her jealous evident in the wink he shot her before he walked off. "You coming?" he hollered to Trevor. "We've got 'non-lame' stuff to set up."

"In a minute," Trevor said, never taking his eyes off me. He hooked his thumbs in his jeans' pockets, which pulled his already snug T-shirt even tighter across his impressive chest, then he flipped his bangs out of his face. "Need a ride? I could swing by on my bike."

I could feel my face flame purple. My parents would never let me go to a party unsupervised, even if it was just a group of kids hanging out and having a bonfire--especially with the increased crime lately. They'd be worried we'd burn down the woods or, worse, ourselves. They might be right, but I didn't want to sound like I was a kid that needed my parent's permission by saying no.

"Oh, well, I--"

"Yes, she does," Mel cut me off. "Maria and I have our own bikes, but Sam's broke."

"It did not ... ow! That's right, it did." Maria winced, adjusting her feet beneath the table. "Flat tire."

"Pick you up at five?" Trevor asked.

"Oh, well, it won't take an hour to ... ow! Five is good." I glared at Mel, then squinted up at Trevor. "I'm staying with my dad this week, so meet me at the end of Main Street."

Trevor nodded once, then jogged off to catch up to the football team. I tried not to drool as I watched the pockets of his jeans shift with every step.

"Told you I was right," Mel said. "He just asked you out."

"He did not ask me out. He offered me a ride. We're all going to be in trouble if we get caught, you know."

"We're just hanging out with friends, Sam. Try to enjoy yourself. Think about it. He's picking you up an hour early," Maria added. "It's not that long of a bike ride to the party. This is way more than an offer of a ride."

"What if he's just being nice? What if I faint? I don't want to make a fool of myself. What do I do?"

"You relax and quit stressing." Mel patted my hand. "No matter what you say, it is a date. Him giving you a ride there gives you a little time alone."

"I guess you're right, but here's an even bigger question ... what do I wear?"

"We've got Maria," Mel said. "We can't go wrong."

"Let's go, girls!" Maria grinned. "We've got some shopping to do."

12

TRICK OR ... TRICK!

"Nice costume," Trevor said, adjusting the cape on his vampire outfit.

"Thanks. You, too," I responded, gathering my black witch's dress in my hands. I had wanted to be a princess, but Maria had found out Trevor was going to be a vampire and insisted a witch's costume was the better choice. Only I'd forgotten we'd be riding a bike.

"Hop on." He gripped the handlebars of his trick bike.

"So, these are your wheels?" I stood on the pegs attached to the sides of his back tire, holding onto his broad shoulders.

He shrugged. "It's not much. When I get my license, I'm getting a truck. My dad says that way I won't have a ton of my friends distracting me." Trevor glanced at me quick, then back at the road. "One person can be way more distracting than a bunch."

"Really?" What did I say to that? I still wasn't convinced this was anything more than him giving me a ride to the party. I didn't want to fall for him only to get my heart broken.

"Yeah, really." He turned on a side road and headed in a direction I had never been.

"This isn't the way to the OC road." I tried not to hyperventilate. "Aren't we running late?"

"Want to stop and talk first? Have that rain check you mentioned?" He pulled his bike off the road and parked in the empty lot with the fantastic view off the cliff of a lake nestled in a clearing.

I hopped down and sat on a large boulder. "Trevor, I--"

He sat down beside me and held up his hand. "It's not what you think."

"It's not?" I didn't know whether to be relieved or disappointed. "I don't understand."

"I'm not making much sense." He shoved a hand through his shoulder-length curls and let out a breath. "I really like you."

"You do?"

"Yeah. You make me laugh." He lowered his eyes. "I haven't really dated much, either." His gaze met mine. "But every time I try to talk to you, you take off." He stuffed his hands in his pockets. "I'm not sure how to read you."

"You're not alone." I let out the breath I'd been holding. "We've moved around so much, I don't date. But I, um, really like you, too."

"You do?" He looked surprised.

I smiled shyly. "Yeah. You get me."

"Cool." He exhaled loudly, sounding relieved.

This awkward silence filled the air around us, and I swear the birds even stopped squawking. The temperature outside rose by three point five degrees, according to my internal thermometer. With my luck, I'd set the woods on fire.

"What did you want to ask me the other day?" I asked.

"On a date, but I guess we kind of are," he said.

He was as nervous as I was, and it allowed me to relax a little. Then, I channeled my inner superhero and let confidence fill me.

"Oh, well, I don't know. <u>Are</u> we on a date? I thought dates involved going somewhere and you giving me something like a gift."

A slow lopsided grin formed on his adorable face. "If someone would stop running away from me, I could have planned a little better."

"I'm here now. What would you normally do?"

"I'd pick you up and take you somewhere nice."

I glanced at his bike and then out at the fabulous view. "Check and check." I laughed.

The other corner of his mouth tipped up a hair. "Then we would talk for a while."

I tapped my cheek with my finger. "Hmmm, I'd say that's another check."

He looked at my mouth and cleared his throat. "What was the last thing you mentioned?"

"That you'd give me something like a gift."

His brows crept up, his face just inches from mine. "You're not going to run away again, are you?" His voice dipped lower.

"No."

He closed the space between us, lowering his head carefully and tipping his face to the side. I swear my eyes rolled in the back of my head, and he hadn't even touched me yet. He wrapped his arms around me, and I could feel his breath on my face only inches away. This was it. He was finally going to kiss me. I touched the strands of his hair like I'd been dying to do for so long. His palm settled awkwardly on my shoulder, he leaned in closer, and....

A mix of pain and pleasure seared my skin. Heat burned a path through my cells, straight to my GPS brain, my mind's eye exploding with white light once again.

I screamed loud and long.

"What'd I do?" He jumped, and we both fell off the rock. He lay on his back in the dirt with both his hands in the air as though I had a gun pointed at him.

"My head again." I blinked against the massive headache hammering my temples as I straightened my black dress. I scrunched my eyes closed against the bright flash of light and phone number that lingered in my eyes.

"Maybe you should have that checked," he said, and I opened my eyes to see the wary look on his face.

"Good idea." Heat and tingling coursed down my spine, straight to my legs, and my body jerked into motion like I feared it would.

"Right now?" He gaped at me as I stood and started to walk away from him. "What about the party?"

"I'll catch the next one. Thanks for the date." I held on tight to my bag.

"Sam, wait!" I heard him say as he scrambled to his feet, but I had already disappeared into the woods. "Sam? Come on, this isn't funny. Where'd you go?" His voice drifted farther away, then I heard him get back on his bike and ride off.

"Just great," I muttered, as my feet guided me. I changed out of my witch's costume and into my superhero disguise along the way. Why did this keep happening to me when I was with Trevor? Was the universe was against us dating each other? Why couldn't these episodes happen around the Burdick Twins: two doofuses I'd gladly run away from?

I gasped. Because they didn't send my hormones soaring like Trevor did. This was the worst case scenario possible.

These episodes weren't just about me ... they were about Trevor.

He was my trigger.

Every time he was around me, my hormones rose to the boiling point on my Love Meter. A signal must shoot from my cell hand to the 911 tower I was tapped into, blocking a random 911 call. Then my lovely GPS brain would reroute me, sending Gamma Girl to the rescue.

Those poor people. Thank God no one had been seriously hurt, especially with the recent increase in crime.

This was so unfair. I was so close to finally getting what I wanted more than anything else: Trevor Hamilton to kiss me. Dealing with my uniqueness was hard enough to handle without adding Gamma Girl episodes. I couldn't believe I was thinking this, but I had no choice. I had to avoid Trevor Hamilton, and say goodbye to the best thing I 'almost' ever had.

"You've got to be kidding me. Please don't take me there!" I fought to make my legs stop moving, or at the very least to turn in the other direction, but I had no control over them.

I resigned myself to my fate as I looked up and stared at the street sign I'd just turned on. O'Connor Road. The dead end road that bordered Farmer Johnson's property.

The Halloween party site!

Fear hit me. After Mrs. Lipowitz's garage was ransacked, and Frat Boy's dorm was set on fire, I was a little worried about what I'd find here.

"There he is!" Maria screeched, then squinted at the front of my costume. I'd written my superhero name in marker, hoping it would help. "Granny Grunt? Oh-kay, whatever. At least you're here." She squealed, jumping up and down in her Little Bo Peep outfit and clapping her hands. "I knew you'd come."

Granny Grunt? Okay, third time was definitely <u>not</u> the charm. "It's Gamma Girl, Maria, can't you read? And what are you doing, calling 911?" I asked, not thinking.

She stopped hopping and scrunched up her face. "Wait, you sound familiar. How did you know my name?"

"Earth to Peep Head. You called 911 and gave your name," Mel, dressed as Frankenstein's bride, came to my rescue. "She knows my name, too, don't you Gammy?"

"I do?" I lowered my voice to a deeper, husky tone so Gamma Girl would sound different than Samantha. But I was having a hard time focusing. Trevor sat by the fire, moving the wood around with a stick, looking distant and unapproachable. I felt bad that I had done that to him. He'd never forgive me now. I'd never forgive myself. I just wanted this whole thing to be over.

"Yes, you do," Mel interrupted my thoughts. "Remember you came to the rescue when my brother called?"

"I did?" I tried to peer around her and through the growing crowd of students to see Trevor better, but he wasn't paying attention to me.

"Then how come none of us heard about that blocked call," Ali asked in her Cat Woman costume, looking skeptical and yet admittedly fantastic at the same time.

"Because my brothers are dorks. Twins usually are." Mel smirked at the Burdick Bozos who wore Bart and Homer Simpson costumes and towered over Ali like two bodyguards. "I didn't want anyone to know that one of them super glued the remote to the other one's hand. Not a problem normally, but I was babysitting and my favorite show was on in five minutes. They knew they were dead if they didn't get it off. Who knew nail polish remover would work like a charm? Right Gammy?"

"It's Gamma Girl, and uh, right." I refocused on Maria. "Who needs help this time?"

"And you guys called me lame?" Big Matt the Samurai Warrior said. "Who calls 911 over cow tipping?"

My jaw fell open. "Cow what-ing?"

"Nope he's definitely not from around here if he doesn't know what cow tipping is," Matt said.

"She!" I snapped. I didn't care anymore. I was tired of all of this.

"<u>She</u> doesn't get out much," Mel muttered.

"Never mind that. Who's hurt," I said. "I have other people to help, you know." I just wanted to get this over and leave.

"The cow, of course," Maria added. "The big ape here tipped the poor cow over, and it never got up. I think it's dead."

"It's not dead. It's just sleeping," Simon dressed as Albert Einstein said as he joined our growing circle. "It'll be fine when it wakes up. You don't have to worry, Mel."

"Trust me, I could care less." Mel rolled her eyes.

"Simon, you made it." Maria ignored Mel's glare. "I'm glad. What would we have done without you?"

Simon shrugged, never taking his eyes off Mel. Boys were so clueless.

"<u>You</u> invited him?" Mel whispered to Maria. "Are you crazy?"

Maria pouted, crossing her arms and not saying a word.

"Since I'm no longer needed, I'll be on my way." I turned to leave.

"Not so fast." Ali grabbed my shoulder and spun me

around. "I think it's time we all got to know you a little better. Daddy's reward money would let us throw a real party. Who's with me?"

"Get to know who better?" Trevor stepped into the circle. His gaze dropped to the front of my sparkly costume, and his eyes narrowed.

Ali glared. "Some superhero she is. She didn't <u>do</u> anything. Simon here saved the day. If you ask me, this chick is just a poser. I think it's about time we found out who she really is." She stepped back, never one to do her own dirty work. "Boys. Unmask the fraud."

"Wait." Trevor stepped forward.

I shook out my hands and adjusted my matching pink and purple sparkly mask as a confidence only Gamma Girl could give flooded my system. I had no choice but to stand my ground.

His gaze grew even more intense as he studied me. "Do I know you? Something seems familiar."

"Absolutely not." My eyes never left Trevor's. "I <u>am</u> a superhero, after all ... that's the only thing you need to know about me." I let a teasing smile play across my lips. Where was this confidence coming from? I was pretty sure Gamma Girl was the reason, and I was loving it.

"Superhero? I don't think so." Burdick One lunged for my mask.

My brain fired up my neurons, the left side calculating the exact move he was going to make. My motor neurons warped down my spine, carrying my brain's message to move. My adrenalin charged limbs didn't hesitate as they dodged in the right direction, stepping out of the way like an experienced matador outmaneuvering a bull.

"Ole," came flying out of my mouth.

"O-what?" He scratched his head. "Sit back and let me

show you how it's done." Ugh. My body froze like a wax statue. "In a minute, that is." My Electro Wave chose that moment to reboot, my entire central nervous system locking up as my body whirred and hummed. I literally couldn't move; I was paralyzed.

"Problems, Gammy?" Mel asked, sounding nervous. "You look constipated. Now is not the time to freeze up. Trust me, you need movement, pronto!"

I looked up and saw Burdick Two moving into position. "Hang on ... just restarting ..."

He grinned evilly and lunged from a different direction. My forebrain, midbrain and hindbrain finished updating at the last second, and my body surged to life once more. I sidestepped in the nick of time.

Faster than the speed of light, I watched a Google demonstration about mixed martial arts on the back of my retinas, leaving me momentarily light-headed. After channeling my hindbrain to regulate my balance, movement and coordination, my neurons carried the information down my spine to the necessary limbs, and my head cleared.

I executed a perfect drop kick to his backside, and one of my boots flew off, whacking Ali in the head, sending her face first in the dirt. "Whoops sorry." Ignoring her scowl, I snatched my boot and yanked it back on as I said to Burdick Two, "Take that, nimrod!"

The crowd cheered, distracting me, and Ali screeched as she ran over and yanked my hat and mask off. Everyone stared, stunned. I didn't move. I couldn't.

"Sam?" Trevor gaped at me.

"Surprise!" I laughed, wanting to cry but relieved my secret was out. I couldn't take the pressure anymore.

"No way," said Ali. "She can't be the real superhero. She doesn't have the guts."

I gaped at her. "Are you kidding? You unmasked me yourself, and I'm wearing the costume."

"So are those five kids who just showed up. Gamma Groupies ... you guys all make me sick."

I whirled around and sure enough, several kids had just shown up dressed in their versions of what they thought the superhero might look like. Crazy colors and styles thrown together with the names Harry Weird or Supper Flask written across the chest. The media hadn't captured the superhero on film yet, and there were mixed reports on what the superhero looked like and if there was more than one.

I starting giggling hysterically and couldn't stop. This was crazy, insane, ridiculous.

"Shows over, guys. They're all posers," Ali spat as she stomped away.

Trevor stared at me, looking confused and hurt.

"I had a spare costume?" I said, sounding lame to my own ears.

"Guess soccer and school aren't the only things you're good at," he said quietly. "If you didn't want to go to the party with me all you had to do was say so."

"Trevor, I--"

He held up his hand, his face unreadable once more. "Save it." He turned and walked away.

The cluster of Gamma Groupies spotted me, heading my way with huge smiles. I couldn't deal with this right now.

"Um, remember, stay out of trouble, don't do drugs, don't drink and drive ... yadda, yadda, yadda." Superheroes gave good messages, yet everyone stare at me like I was whacked.

Everyone except the Gamma Groupies. "Right on, man," they shouted and cheered, fist pumping the air. Of course there were no girls among them. Figured. Then again, maybe it was a good thing everyone thought the superhero was a boy. The last thing I needed was someone to point the finger at me.

"Right. You take care, kids," I tried again. "Um ... up, up and away." I thrust a fist in the air, which got a few odd stares, and made Trevor take another wary step back. "Hulk Smash? Flame On? Shazam?" They still just stared, and I tossed up my hands. "Holy whatever, Batman, I've got to bail."

I marched off, hearing the Gamma Groupies holler where you going and Trevor mutter something about, 'Girls! Who needs them?' I'd have to work on a parting phrase for the next time, if there was a next time. But at least I'd accomplished one goal.

Getting Trevor Hamilton to hate me.

13

LICENSE TO RESCUE

I'd no sooner left the party and hit the main road, when a dark sedan with tinted windows pulled up behind me and slowed down. When it didn't pass, I got spooked. I should never have crossed the main road to head back for my bag.

Turning around, I darted onto Farmer Johnson's property, hoping to lose the car. Ten minutes later, after zigzagging across the pasture, I no longer heard a car. Just to be sure, I stopped and looked. I'd read in the instruction manual I was still struggling to get through that this cell phone came equipped with night vision. The Electro Wave sure wasn't like any cell phone I'd used before. At this moment, I couldn't be more grateful.

Squeezing my eyes tight for three seconds, I enabled the night vision feature. My eyeballs burned. When I opened my eyelids, everything around me was ultra dark ... except for two forms illuminated in green. Maybe they were just animals. It was hard to tell, so I pressed my temples and the heat sensors clicked on, shooting intense heat from one temple to the other, highlighting the forms in the distance in red.

Human forms.

Two large bodies--one tall, one short--moved across the pasture, tracking the exact path I'd taken. Something told me they weren't your average tourist trying to get a peek at the superhero.

I spun around and ran, steam hissing out my ears and the taste of jalapeño peppers coating my tongue. I was only a thirteen-year-old girl. There was no way I could outrun them. Air burned my lungs as I pumped my arms and legs faster. I could feel them, I could sense them ... oh God, I could hear them.

I broke through a clearing, sending a few cows scattering and a flock of birds soaring into the air. Then I saw the most beautiful sight. Farmer Johnson's tractor. A huge yellow combine with tons of controls. I was scared, but I had help.

My brain whizzed and roared as it downloaded the operating manual, gears grinding and the wheels in my head spinning at high speed. Concentrating hard, I sent the information soaring down my spine, straight to my fingertips which grew a half inch. Freaky. I glanced down to see if anything else on me had grown.

Of course I couldn't be that lucky.

Focusing on my task, I broke a nail as I hotwired the tractor's engine and fired up the beast within seconds after I reached her. Minutes later, I had her moving at top speed. The international harvester might not be fast, but it was definitely faster than my stalkers.

Once those men reached their car, they'd be searching the streets for me. I planned to ditch the tractor as soon as I hit the edge of Farmer Johnson's property. It took me twenty minutes to reach the road, and by that time, I found two more men waiting for me. Men scarier than my stalkers.

Farmer Johnson and Sheriff Hamilton.

I cut the engine and climbed down off the monstrous combine, trying to think of a way out of this mess.

"Sheriff, I demand this thief be arrested." Farmer Johnson stabbed a finger in my direction as he stomped his foot. "Youngins' these days have no respect for other people's properties."

"I'm not a thief, sir, I promise. I was just borrowing your tractor. I would never steal anything," I quickly said.

"Relax, Bobby, he's just a kid." Sheriff Hamilton swiped a hand over his face and turned to me.

Grrr on the "he" again.

"That's no kid, Nate. That's one of them superheroes. Trouble seems to follow him wherever he goes, and I don't want no trouble on my property. I can't afford to get robbed like the Widow Lipowitz, and I sure as heck can't afford for my barn to get set on fire like that college boy." He scoffed. "Heck, this kid is probably the one causing all the problems around here."

"I swear I'm not causing trouble. I'm not even one of the real superheroes. This is just my Halloween costume for a party I was supposed to go to." I whipped off my mask, my heart pounding and throat dry. It had worked at the party. I just hoped it worked here.

"See, it's just me. Samantha Granger. You know how crazy my mom gets when I'm late, Sheriff. No harm done, right? I promise I'll never do anything like this again, Mr. Johnson. I really am sorry. Can I go now?"

"You're about the thirtieth superhero I've seen tonight," Sheriff Hamilton said, and I nearly fell to the ground with relief that he believed me. He shook his head. "I can't let you go anywhere. You're still in a lot of trouble, Sam. You could have been seriously hurt, driving something this big and complicated. At the very least I'm going to have to call your parents. As far as the rest goes, that's up to Farmer Johnson on whether or not he wants to press charges."

I chewed my lip and stared at the farmer, pleading with my eyes.

"You bet yer booty, I'm gonna press charges. She didn't 'borrow' Big Bertha like she claims. There were no keys. The girl hotwired my baby--that sure does sound like intent to steal." He plopped his hat on his head and saluted the Sheriff. "I expect justice, Nate." He climbed up in his combine and drove back to his farm without looking back.

I was being arrested? My parents were going to flip. I'd dodged a bullet with Gamma Girl's real identity, but I still had to deal with the wrath of my parents. I didn't know which was scarier. "What happens now, Sheriff? Do you really have to take me to jail?"

"Looks that way. Sorry Sam." He studied me like he could see right through me. Finally, he said in a quiet, serious voice, "But first you tell me exactly where that party is, and who's there."

And just like that my life was over.

"Thank you so much for dropping the charges, Bobby," Gram patted Farmer Johnson's arm as we stood outside the police station. Leave it to Gram to know half the town already.

Ali drove by with her father, her face plastered to the window of their car. The news would be everywhere in seconds.

Farmer Johnson flushed bright pink but didn't move away from Gram's hand. "Why, I had no idea she was your granddaughter, Gabby. Still, she could've wrecked my Bertha or, even worse, hurt herself."

"You're absolutely right." Gram glanced in my direction with a stern disapproving look, then smiled as sweet as pie back up at the farmer. "Don't you worry; she will be punished. In the meantime, please accept this peach cobbler as a thank you. I know it's your favorite." They walked off to the parking lot together, heads bent close, talking nonstop.

Mom turned around once they were out of earshot and glared at Dad. "This is your fault, Wally. If you were any kind of father, this wouldn't have happened."

"My fault? You're the one she's been living with, Victoria. Looks like I arrived just in time." Dad glared back.

"It was your weekend. She was at your house when it happened. Look at that rash. She's going to need to see a doctor." They had no idea the rash was a side effect from downloading that tractor video. No doctor could cure what ailed me.

"Fine, I take full responsibility." He sighed, sounding tired as he squeezed the bridge of his nose.

"Good. Then you deal with her punishment. I'm late." Mom hurried after Gram, who waited by her car, crossing her arms and tapping her foot.

Mom was in as much trouble as I was, I thought, relieved at having Dad be the one to punish me. I gave him my sweetest Daddy's little girl smile.

"Get in, hotshot." We climbed in his Prius, but he didn't say a word until we pulled into the empty parking lot at Electro Corp.

"What are we doing here?" I asked.

He climbed out of the car and switched sides with me. "You think driving is so easy, then go for it. Driving a tractor in a pasture is a whole lot different than driving a car on the road."

Mom had been furious, as usual, and insisted Dad teach me a lesson. His idea of a lesson involved teaching me how to drive for real to be sure I was safe. At thirteen I should be petrified to get behind the wheel. After all the crazy things I'd been through lately, driving a car in an empty parking lot ranked pretty low on my scare meter.

I was more afraid nobody would like me after showing up with Sheriff Hamilton at the party on O.C. road. I'd tried to lead him on a wild goose chase, but the man knew the area too well. He'd figured it out all on his own, but nobody believed I hadn't ratted them out. Now no one would talk to me, except Mel of course. Just wait until they found out I'd been arrested. I groaned.

"Well, what are you waiting for?" Dad asked in his best stern father voice, but he wasn't fooling anyone. We both knew Mom wore the pants, separation or no separation.

"I know what I did was wrong, Dad. I was just afraid Mom would have a cow if I was late. Ever since you two split, she's more uptight than ever."

"Being a single parent hasn't been easy for her," he said quietly, "but I'm back now, and so is Gram. That should help."

"Back for good as in maybe we can all be a family again?" I asked, trying not to be so obvious about my hope.

"Samantha, you know that's not going to happen."

"Whatever." I shrugged.

"What happened to that rash?" He inspected my arms.

"Gone, I guess." I pulled away. "You do know I can't drive

for three more years, right?" I asked, hoping to distract him from my miraculous recovery.

"It's never too early to start learning," he answered, sounding just as happy about changing the subject.

"Mom would freak if she knew."

"Don't worry about Mom, just concentrate. It's okay to admit you're nervous. I just want to make sure you're safe. Driving a car for the first time can be intimidating." He took a few breaths, even though we weren't going anywhere except a few parking spaces over. "Let's start with the different parts that make up a car. Do you know any of the parts of a car?"

I straightened in my seat--head tipping, nose twitching, and lips puckering--as the wheels in my mind cranked and churned. After mere seconds, I spit out every single part both inside and out of the very car we sat in.

Dad sat stunned. "How did ... when ... where ... what the heck was that?"

"Motor vehicles. Secret hobby," I said. Now I was nervous.

"Now that we've established you know your way around cars as much as tractors, let's see if you can drive one."

He started to go over the operating manual, but I fired up the engine, startling him into silence. I flipped on my turn signal, checked all my mirrors, looked over my shoulder, and pulled out of the parking spot without missing a beat. After circling the building, executing a perfect three point turn, and parallel parking with pinpoint accuracy, I cut the engine and peeked up at my dad.

"Another hobby?" He stared at me like he didn't know me.

"Video games?" I answered in question format again. I had to stop doing that.

"Which you're obviously spending way too much time playing," he mumbled, slipping out of the car to switch spots with me. "Lesson over." We headed home in silence, him staring straight ahead, not taking his eyes off the road, wearing a dazed and perplexed look.

I had to distract him. "Look at the traffic. Blue Lake never gets this many people in town for the Apple Festival. Won't that help the economy?" I tried to make idle conversation to keep his mind off my textbook driving skills.

"And Congressman Tucker's campaign," he said. "I heard the Apple Festival is one of his many fundraisers, but I don't think that's what drew these people here."

"Then what did?"

"Granny Grunt or whatever the latest name is," he said in a strangely serious voice. "People are starting to get worried, Sam. I'm starting to get worried. They think this group of superheroes is a dangerous gang of sorts."

"Dangerous gang? Whoever he, she, or they are, I think they're harmless," I said. "I mean, they help people."

"Funny how all these crimes started happening right after the first superhero showed up. Farmer Johnson was furious that kids were messing around so close to his property. I'm sure that's the end of parties on the O.C. road. And late last night, one of Electro's warehouses was broken into and vandalized. The police think these crimes might be connected somehow."

"Huh, I never thought of that." I hadn't told the sheriff about the two men who followed me, and I didn't dare tell my dad now. But I made a note to look into the crimes that had happened, and the people they'd happened to. Something even stranger than me turning into a superhero was going on, and I couldn't help thinking maybe they were somehow related.

"Something's going on with you, Sam. Is it the divorce?"

"Separation."

"Honey, your mom and I both told you none of this is your fault."

"Yeah, but you never told me what happened to you at work ... or why you're here." I held my breath, waiting to hear if he'd mention Dark Shades Man and put my fears to rest.

"You don't need to worry about any of that. And you don't need to act out to get our attention. We're still a family, and we're still here for you."

"I'm not acting out, Dad. You know me better than that. A little trust here would be nice."

"You're thirteen, princess." He took a deep breath. "You've never given me a reason not to trust you, but you've been acting strange lately. Going to parties in the woods," he glanced at me, "I have ears. Borrowing tractors. Lord knows what else went on? I'm not ready for any of this."

"Who is? I'm not ready for half the stuff that's been happening to me lately. That's life, I guess."

"What stuff?" He looked at me with a worried expression. No way would I bring up kissing Trevor.

"You, Mom, the move, and ... um ... female stuff."

"Say no more." He sat red faced. Gram always said the best way to shut a man up was to mention female problems, and bingo, end of conversation. I wondered if it would work on boys, too.

"Your mom and I have decided to take you to a doctor. We've noticed some strange ticks you've adopted, and you've hung out in your room all week. You won't even take any of that nice boy, Trevor Hamilton's, phone calls. Didn't your grandmother tell me you had a crush on him?"

<u>Thanks Gram</u>. "I've been having trouble in school, so I've been studying more."

"I thought your grades were better than ever?"

"Most of the time, but like I said, it was a rough week. Female problems, remember?"

"Right." He got quiet for a moment, then asked, "Did something more happen at that party I should know about?" He cleared his throat. "I'm here if you want to talk, female problems or not."

Ewww. I didn't want to have that talk with him any more than he did. That's what moms were for. Or in my case, Grams. "I'm fine, Dad."

"Just the same, we've scheduled you for some neurological tests. Gram tried to tell us you have a photographic memory like hers, but I'd feel more comfortable ruling everything else out."

He pulled back into his driveway, and I was speechless. Terrified. Neurological tests? I couldn't let a doctor look inside my brain. I had to find some way to get out of those tests, or a way to reverse my uniqueness before I was toast.

"What's Mom doing here?" I asked as we got out of the car.

"I'm not sure." Dad scratched his head. "You look as perfect as ever," he said as he came to a stop by her side.

"And you look like ... well, you." Mom smiled. "We have another emergency meeting," she said in a funny voice.

"Ah," he lowered his tone to match hers, "then we'd better check it out. You driving this time or am I?"

<u>This time?</u> "You're riding together?" I blurted.

"We have some things to discuss." Dad's eyes darted to hers, and they exchanged a meaningful look. "The car is more private than the office. Gram is inside if you need anything."

"Okay," I said, watching them drive off together. Something was up. The divorce wasn't settled yet. Maybe they were trying to work things out. Maybe Dad coming back for work was just a front to win Mom back. What if it was actually working?

Looked like I wasn't the only one with secrets.

14

WANNABE SIDEKICK

Heading into my garage, I chose the backyard rather than inside. I wasn't ready to face Gram. My life had spun out of control. I sat on a swing. If I could change things, I would. I never would have walked home from Mel's house a couple weeks ago, and I definitely wouldn't have touched that stupid crystal.

My hand vibrated. What now, I wondered. I glanced around but didn't see anyone, so I slipped my glove off and pressed my palm against my ear. "Hey, Mel, what's up?"

"Scott says Trevor is upset and confused over you being hot then cold. I'm confused. Why won't you return his calls?"

"I thought everyone was mad about me ruining the party?"

"They're over it, especially since you got in more trouble than they did. You're going to mess this up."

"It's already messed up, and there's nothing I can do about it. I want to talk to Trevor so bad, but I can't. According to my owner's manual--don't ask--hormonal fluctuations can cause short circuits to my system." I adjusted my seat on the swing, feeling hopeless as I pictured all the disasters that had happened to me.

"The science guys make me afraid, and that sets off security alarms," I continued. "While Trevor makes me feel all weird inside, and that blocks 911 calls. Can you imagine what will happen if he actually does kiss me? I need to keep my hormones under control, and the only way I can do that is by avoiding him. At least until I find a cure or a way to control my powers. If I don't start acting normal again, my parents are going to send me for some brain scans."

"What are you going to do?"

"The only thing I can. Stay as far away from Trevor as possible."

"Good luck with that because Scott just told me Trevor--"

"Who you talking to?" Trevor asked from behind me, then pushed my swing before I could jump off.

"Eeeek," I screamed, grabbing onto the chains. I somehow managed to disconnect from Mel and slip my glove back on while trying not to have a heart attack.

"Sorry, didn't mean to scare you. Just curious who you're talking to since it's definitely not me." His jaw clamped shut.

He jerked the swing to a dead stop so I fell back against him and had to look up into the greenest most amazing frustrated eyes I'd ever seen. I almost sighed, but then he spoke, reminding me of what I had to do.

"What gives, Sam?" he asked.

"Could you let me down? The blood's rushing to my head," I croaked.

The blood rush didn't have anything to do with hanging upside down. It had to do with the way he made me feel. I wondered if getting zapped had heightened all my senses, instead of just giving me freaky abilities. All this guy had to do was look at me.

"Answer the question," he said quietly.

I practiced my deep breathing, striving for calm. This was ridiculous. "It's not you, it's me."

"You're really going there?" He shoved his hands through his hair and then plopped them on his hips. "This is why I don't ask girls out."

"Trevor, I'm so sorry." I touched his arm, and we both flinched over the electricity that sizzled between us. I started to pull my hand away, but he grabbed my wrist.

"Don't." His eyes searched mine.

I pulled my hand away and stepped back. "You don't understand. My heart's pounding." Seventy four breaths. My systolic rose eight points.

"Mine too. How is that a problem?" He took a step toward me, and I stepped back even more.

"I-I can't," I managed to get out. "I'm not ready."

He stared at me for a long minute. "Wow. Someone or something really did a number on you."

"Some <u>thing</u> sure did. That's why I need more time. Don't you get that?"

He scrubbed his hands over his face. "Why do you have to be this way? I know you like me, too, or you wouldn't let me do this." He pulled me to him and his head swooped down.

I turned my face at the last second and his lips brushed my cheek. Just that simple contact made heat surge through my body and my skin tingle all over. It made me feel special. It made me feel alive.

It made me hurt like heck!

I grabbed my head. "I told you this wasn't a good idea, but you wouldn't listen." I stumbled away from his touch. "I can't see you again, Trevor." I gasped, snatching my bag just in time before my traitorous body propelled me into the woods.

"I give up. I could care less if I ever see you again," he hollered from behind me, not bothering to try to stop me.

My heart broke as I realized I'd just lost the most important thing in my life. Just as I'd feared, I'd been hurt by someone I cared about once again. Even worse, I'd hurt him back.

And it was all my fault.

EXHAUSTED AND DEPRESSED, I KNEW I COULDN'T GO ON THIS way much longer. This time the blocked call came from some teenage girl. She'd backed over a fire hydrant, right into a flag pole at the high school.

Water shot up through her convertible, showering the marching band's blow-up mascot that someone had stolen and strung up the flagpole. Not exactly 911 worthy in my book. These people would call 911 for any reason, and I had better things to do with my time than be sent to their rescue.

"What is wrong with you?" I snapped.

The girl stepped out of her car, looking like a frazzled blonde Barbie doll. "I-I don't know. There was this car. I'm new to driving a stick shift, and the car ran me right off the road. I was supposed to take my dad's car, but my mom insisted I take hers to get more practice."

Alarm prickled my flesh. "What kind of car?"

Her eyes grew huge as she stared just beyond my head. "That kind of car!" Blonde Barbie pointed to the same dark sedan that had chased me through Farmer Johnson's fields. "What do we do?"

"I don't know. You're the older one."

"You're the superhero!" She stared at my chest and scrunched up her nose. "What kind of name is Cellular? At least your other little gang members were more creative with Harry Weird, Supper Flask and Granny Grunt."

Ugh. Someone finally gets my name right, and she thinks I'm lame. Let her try being me. "Trade ya?" I smiled brightly, almost hysterically.

"Trade what?" she shrieked, and I could see the panic welling within her.

"Never mind." I wanted my life back, but that wasn't going to happen if those thugs got a hold of me. "Run!" I yelled, and we took off toward the woods.

One tall dark-skinned guy climbed out of the car, followed quickly by a short dark-skinned guy, but they didn't chase us. All they seemed to care about was breaking into the back of the wrecked convertible. We disappeared under the cover of trees as I heard them speaking rapidly in a funny accent.

That had been way too close.

I left her by the side of a main road she knew, instructing her to call for a ride. I had something I needed to do, and I knew who I had to call. Simon. He was a whiz at computers, and he'd been at that seminar on electromagnetic fields. I sort of understood how I'd absorbed the Electro Wave, but I didn't understand how all my superhero powers worked. I had a feeling Simon could help me put the pieces together.

I called from my cell hand where the caller ID would read Cellular, allowing me to keep my identity a secret. We arranged to meet at his house since no one was home.

A little while later, I stood at his front door. "Hey, Simon, what's up?" I tried to act casual.

"I'm confused," he replied, getting right to the point.

"About what?" I stalled.

"You, me, here ... why?" He scratched his head.

I sighed. "Can I come in?"

He stepped back and let me in.

"You're a genius, okay? Kids at school might not appreciate that, but I do. Right now I need your help."

He puffed up his chest, looking pleased, but then asked, "Why are you wearing the same outfit Sam was at the Halloween party?"

"Because Sam and Mel really do know me," I blurted.

He looked skeptical, but seemed to buy my story. "If I help you, what's in it for me?"

I should have known helping me wouldn't be prize enough. "What do you want?"

"A date with Mel."

Mel was going to kill me, but she'd asked to be a sidekick and that meant helping the superhero out. Right now I needed all the help I could get. "I can probably do that, though I can think of someone else you'd have a much better shot with."

"Nope. Has to be Mel."

"Are you sure there's nothing else you'd rather have?" He shook his head, and I sighed. "Fine. I can set up the date, but the rest is up to you," I added. "I can't make her like you if she doesn't." I looked him over and said gently. "You could help your cause a lot if you'd put some effort into it."

He frowned. "Into what?"

I glanced at his eyes and thought Maria was right. They were the most unusual color. His teeth were so white and straight, he could model for a toothpaste commercial. "I know how hard it is to fit in, but maybe it would be easier if you got a haircut, and went shopping. You know, clean up a bit. You have great potential." I smiled. "You just need to show everyone." I could see why Maria was fascinated by him. Too bad he was too blind to notice.

His face flushed red. "Guess I never thought much about how I looked, but maybe you have a point. Anyway, what did you need me to do?"

"Help give me some answers, and then hack into a computer."

His eyes narrowed, but I saw a spark of interest. "I've seen what you can do."

"I might have access to the Internet, but that doesn't mean I understand it all or that I'm a good hacker. Besides, I will be on a mission, so I'll need someone to man the base."

"What are you up to? And who are you, anyway?"

"I'd tell you, but then I'd have to kill you." I grinned.

"Funny." He smirked. "Seriously, if you want me to do something illegal, you're going to have to fill me in on all the details."

I chewed my lip, knowing I didn't have a choice. I needed his help, and no one else could pull this job off except him. "I'll tell you what I'm up to, but if you say anything, I'll deny it. Everyone will think you're crazy. Are we clear?"

"Perfectly, boss." His tawny eyes sparkled with excitement, and his lips twitched in an obvious effort not to smile.

I told him everything from the beginning, minus the part about who I really was, and he just stared at me in awe.

"Can I see it?" he finally asked.

I slipped off my glove, and he pulled out his cell.

"What's your number?" he asked.

"You <u>would</u> have to call my cell hand. You're such a boy."

I told him my number, and his fingers moved over his phone as though he had the top score at a video game tournament. My hand vibrated, then glowed the transparent blue-green, and my veins formed the words "unknown caller" on my Caller ID.

"You're not in my contact list," I said.

"I am now." He reached forward and grabbed my wrist to add himself to my palm.

I pulled my hand away and slipped my glove back on, trying not to scratch. "Happy now?"

He grinned.

"What were you doing at that seminar anyway?"

"My uncle is the physicist who gave the seminar on energy force fields. I'm sort of into that stuff." He shrugged. "They say I'm just like him. Even named me after him."

"I can't imagine your family's dinner conversations." I snorted.

"My family doesn't ask, 'How was your day?' They ask things like, 'What's your theory about the universe?' Kind of stinks when you're an only child."

I could relate to the only child thing, but I didn't want to give away my identity. "Kind of stinks when you're the only one of your kind, too. Please tell me you understand how I became a superhero?"

"I've been thinking about your situation for a while. The whole idea of being a superhero fascinates me." He flushed, then continued. "I figure the device must be connected to your spinal cord and brain stem somehow, like they are fused together. So the electrodes of the phone are now integrated with the blood and plasma of your body. You know how your brain sends electronic pulses to your body? Well, I'm guessing that device is communicating messages to your nervous system somehow."

"Ewww, that sounds gross when you say it out loud. But it does make sense."

"Pretty cool if you ask me."

"Not so much when you're the one on the receiving end of those messages and have no control over your body."

"Yeah, but to have all that technology right at your fingertips, literally, would be so awesome. We live in a digital world, and you're like the queen. You know, like a digital teenager."

Digital Diva, I thought, and a warm hum vibrated through my system, releasing feel-good endorphins throughout my body. Somehow the name felt right. "I love it!"

"Love what?" He eyed me warily.

"Never mind. Do you think there's a way to reverse what happened?"

He hesitated. "You're going to think I'm wacked."

"I'm going to think you're wacked? That's funny."

"Okay, here goes. One time on an episode of Star Trek--"

"Star Trek? Are you for real?"

"Just hear me out."

"Fine, beam me up, Simmy, I'm all ears." I smirked.

"Aye aye, Spoc." He laughed. "Hey, you started it. Anyway, I think you need to transfer the energy you gained back into the crystal."

"How am I supposed to do that, Captain?"

"Get a running start and throw yourself onto the sucker."

I gaped at him. "Are you crazy? That sounds painful."

He shrugged. "At this point, isn't it worth a try?"

"I'll do it, but you're so going with me."

"Are you kidding? Being the only person in Blue Lake to go on a mission with the local superhero would rock. Tell me when and where, and I'm there."

"Awesome." I knew exactly how Simon felt with trying to

fit in, to be accepted. "Synchronize your watch with mine," I said.

"Check," he responded.

"It's ten hundred right now. Let's meet back here at twelve hundred. Are you sure your parents won't be home?" I asked.

"They're gone on a wine tour in the Finger Lakes overnight, so they won't be home until tomorrow morning."

"Do you have the right equipment we need?"

"You're kidding right?" He arched a brow.

"Sorry. Stupid question. It's just we've only got one shot at this, and I don't want to blow it."

"I can do this." He saluted me. "So can you. See you at twelve hundred, Captain."

"You do know this really isn't an episode of Star Trek." I laughed.

He stared at my hand. "Close enough."

15

GRAM IS IN THE HOUSE!

"Double D to base camp, Double D to base camp, do you read me?" I asked Simon through my cell hand as I hid in the edge of the woods behind the science lab at Blue Lake University. He was set up twenty feet behind me, with a huge backpack that carried all his gear ... whatever that meant.

"Double D?"

"Short for Digital Diva."

"Nice!"

"I thought so. Anyway, do you read me, or what?"

"Loud and clear, Double D. The S-Man has you covered, over."

"S-Man?"

"You're not the only one who needs a nickname. We need to keep our convo on the down low. My parents find out I'm involved in something like this, they'll take away my computer."

"Been there." I snorted. "Doesn't matter now."

"Lucky you. Is your cell phone fully charged?"

"As long as I'm alive, my phone is always charged."

"Oh, right. Sorry. What's your status?"

I glanced around the area. "All clear. The back entrance of the lab looks deserted. What's the 411 on your end?"

"The men in white coats are out to lunch. Do you have your disguise?"

"Check."

"Gloves? We wouldn't want your fingerprints all over, even though I'd still like to know who you are."

"Still not gonna happen, and check on the gloves."

"And your excuse if you get caught?"

"I was answering a blocked 911 call, but it must have been a prank because no one was here. Then I leave immediately."

"Perfect. You should have thirty minutes before the staff returns from lunch."

"Cool. The guard just left the building," I said, "and some guy is with him. Wait. Dark Shades Man? What's he doing here?"

"Don't know who you're talking about, but they're gone now. We need to move. Countdown to security system shut down in three, two, one ... All system's go! Call if you need me."

"Roger, dodger. Over and out." I disconnected but not before hearing the S-Man chuckling in the background as he said something like, 'and she thinks I'm the goofy one.' I grinned. Simon was actually pretty cool once you got to know him.

I hurried to the back window of the science lab. I just hoped the S-Man was as good as I thought he was. The security system should be off and the door should be unlocked if everything went as planned. I would slip in, find my answers, then slip out.

If this worked, I'd go out with Simon myself.

I tried the door. It opened. Checking the area one more time, I slipped inside and shut the door behind me. I had to turn on the lights since the windows had been taped over. The scientists weren't kidding when they said this investigation was top secret. But I didn't have time to wait.

I was on a mission.

I made my way to the center and stared in awe and a bit of fear at the large crystal that sat on the table before me, surrounded by a quarantined bubble. It still glowed. My palm tingled just looking at it, as though my body remembered that life-altering event. I figured whatever contaminates it had were already inside me, so I should be fine. As fine as a walking piece of technology could be, that is.

I took a minute to scan the room while I got up the nerve to throw myself on the stupid thing. There were all kinds of equipment with various sized chunks of the crystal in different stages of testing. It looked like they had exhausted every kind of test known to man, and each result came back that it was indeed a meteor ... and radioactive. That's why it was still glowing. It was just different than any other meteor they'd ever seen, and they didn't want to panic people until they found a way to contain the meteor and make sure Blue Lake was safe.

I was all for that, totally ready to get back to normal. Rubbing my hands together, I decided to just go for it. Now or never, and all that. I was just about to leap when I noticed a file in the far corner on a desk by a phone. My camera eye zoomed in and locked on a name I knew well. Wally Granger – Electro Case Number 231A. Something inside me was afraid to look in that file, afraid of what I might find, but my need to know ignored the alarm bells going off in my head.

I slowly walked over and opened the top, then stared in

shock at the paper before me. At the picture of a cell phone right next to my dad's name.

"Oh, my God, no," I said as I read page after page in disbelief. Dad was the engineer behind the Electro Wave? He would seriously freak if he knew this Electronic Frankenstein he created was inside my body. An actual part of me now. I vowed then and there that he could never find out.

I read on in horror. They'd made the connection that this superhero must somehow have the Electro Wave, and they were after her to get it back. I shivered. That part was bad enough, but the next section took my breath away. I sat down and flipped the page.

Electro Corp wasn't just a small electronic corporation for consumer purposes. I read on in disbelief. That was a front for Electro's real purpose. It was a government owned and operated corporation with a top secret division that developed highly classified, high tech devices for military use. Mom was in charge of the consumer division. Dad, however, had been in charge of the military division.

The device was not just a cell phone.

"Oh my God," I whispered, trying not to hyperventilate. Mom hadn't given me a new phone; she'd somehow mixed up the boxes and given me a military weapon by mistake. If anyone found out it was inside me, I'd be toast. Speaking of toast, I rubbed my eyes: What if I fried my eyeballs by using the night vision and heat sensors. I inhaled deep and made myself relax. I could still see, so I must be okay. Apparently, I was more than okay.

I was a Billion Dollar Babe!

That explained why Mom was freaking out, wondering where I lost the Electro Wave in the woods. And that definitely explained why Dad had come back. He'd been called in to help. So much for him coming back for Mom and me. The Government wouldn't rest easy until they got their device back. They'd even sent Agent Russell Maxwell to investigate. I studied his picture.

Dark Shades Man.

At least I knew Dad wasn't doing anything illegal, but still, I felt deceived and a little angry. They could have told me. I grabbed the file the government agent had put together and started reading. This whole thing was so much bigger than I'd imagined. No wonder the government was concerned. The recent crime spree wasn't random. They were all connected to Electro.

Mrs. Lipowitz was the widow of a man who was once the chief engineer at Electro. Frat Boy's roommate, Nelson Carmichael, was the son of Electro's weapon's specialist. Blonde Barbie was the daughter of a File Clerk at Electro. Now what? I knew they were all connected, but I still didn't know what these criminals wanted or who was behind it all.

I took pictures of everything with my camera eyes and stored them on my internal hard drive, then I'd make copies on my flash drive later. As soon as I figured out where to stick the memory stick, that is. Hadn't quite gotten to that part of my instruction manual. I shuddered, then focused on the more important issue at hand. Figuring out what these criminals wanted and stopping them from succeeding. At least I knew I wasn't an alien.

I'd take whatever I could get at this point.

SOMETIME LATER I GLANCED AT MY WATCH AND REALIZED I'D lingered too long. I slipped off my glove, careful not to touch anything, and dialed Simon.

"Double D to base camp, do you read me?"

"S-Man here. What took you so long?"

"You wouldn't believe me if I told you. On my way out."

"Did you complete the mission? Are you back to normal?"

"No and no. I'll explain later. Give me two minutes before you turn the alarm system back on, okay?"

"Roger that. Over and--"

"Oh, no."

"What?"

"Someone's coming." I disconnected my cell hand and turned it off completely in case S-Man tried to call at a bad time. Like now! I gulped and dove behind a lab table seconds before Scary Tall Man and Scary Short Man walked through the door.

"What the hell?" the tall, stocky one with curly hair and glasses said in that funny accent again. "They left the door unlocked?"

"Forget that, why didn't the alarm go off?" the short, beefy one with a beard said. "The lights are on. They wouldn't be that careless."

"Something's not right." The tall one swept his coat aside and pulled a gun out of the back waist band of his pants.

I held my breath.

"You check that half of the room, and I'll check this side." Surprise, surprise, the short one had a gun, too.

I started to sweat.

As they moved to the back of the room, I slowly slid on my stomach beneath the desks toward the front. I had almost made it, but my bag got caught. I pulled to free it a little too hard. The entire table slid with it, scraping loudly across the floor.

My head snapped up, and theirs dipped beneath the tables. For a moment, we all froze. Then everything sped up like a movie on high speed as a flurry of motion took place all at once.

"Get her!" the tall one shouted.

"Block the door!" the short one ordered.

"Leave me alone," I screamed, wedging a table between them and me. The door was behind them, and my back was against the wall, literally. "You'll never get away with this. People know me. I'm Digital Diva."

"No one knows your real identity. People will assume Digital Diva disappeared for fear of being discovered, which is understandable since so many tourists have flooded to Blue Lake to get a glimpse of you," the tall one pointed out.

"Yeah. Poor kid couldn't take the pressure," the short one said with a sneer. "It did you in." He grinned menacingly then shoved the table forward, pressing it into my stomach.

"Hey, watch it, buddy, or I'll ... I'll ..."

"What exactly <u>can</u> you do," the tall one asked, and I jumped on the curiosity I saw in his eyes.

"You don't want to find out, buster," I spat, channeling my inner Mel. "I'll fry your butt with my laser beam."

"I'm supposed to believe that?" the short one scoffed, ready to shove the table harder. He obviously didn't want the entire campus to hear a gunshot. My squished guts were much quieter.

I had to do something. I yanked off my glove, but nothing happened. My system froze. Ugh. Probably a stupid virus. I downloaded antivirus software as fast as I could, feeling a rush of cool fluids cleanse my insides, droplets leaking out my tear ducts.

"Is that supposed to be scary?" the tall one said and put

his hands on the table to help. "Looks like you're the one who's scared."

"I wouldn't do that if I were you," I said to stall for time as I wiped my eyes.

"Why, you going to talk us to death? Now, that I would believe." They both laughed.

I used the distraction to give my hand a good whack like my Gram did when our home computer lagged. It worked! My hand came off vibrate, causing it to glow blue-green as the iridescent screen came to life, the heat drying my tears instantly. Then I thrust my palm at them, shouting, "Kablam!"

The short one jumped back. "What is that?"

"Relax, it's just a light," said the tall one, not nearly as impressed. "Fascinating, but hardly deadly. We, on the other hand, are very deadly. The kid knows too much."

"And you know nothing! I have a computer for a brain. It won't take much to outthink you, and I've already called for help. My sidekick has more than just a light. You're going to be sorry you messed with me."

"Somehow, I doubt--" the door burst open and slammed into the backs of both men, whacking them on their heads and dropping them to the floor in two unconscious heaps.

"Ta-Dah! Never fear, S-Man is here," Simon spread his arms wide, then blinked at the men he'd knocked out at his feet. "Did I do that?" he asked in stunned surprise.

"Simon? When I mentioned a sidekick, I was talking about Mel, not you. Who the heck are you supposed to be?" I asked as I scrambled across the top of the table with my bag in tow.

"Captain S-Man," he answered, following close on my heels as we slipped out the door and darted across the back-yard into the woods. He picked up his much lighter backpack minus his "gear" which he now wore, and we sprinted faster.

"You look more like Captain Underpants," I said, unable to stop laughing from nerves and his shocking outfit.

"What did you expect? You tell me someone is coming and then leave me hanging. I couldn't sit back and do nothing."

"My knight in shining ... underwear." I giggled again as we kept moving.

"It's a bathing suit, not underwear, and it's my dad's."

"Ick. Even worse. And the white tights?"

"My mother's." His face turned red, what I could see of it beneath his nylon mask, as I gaped at him but didn't say a word.

He was dressed all in white like Mr. Clean, with his white Speedo, white beater with a capital S & M written in permanent marker on the front, white tights with the feet cut out and flip flops thrown on. He'd even cut up an old sheet and tied it around his neck like a cape. I had to give him an A for effort, but he really did need a style makeover. Big time.

"Beggars can't be choosers." He scowled at me, sounding just like Mel. Maybe they had more in common they I thought.

"You're right, but could you take that nylon off your head? It's a little hard to talk to you like that. What I have to say is serious." He complied, and I grabbed his arms and stopped walking, staring up at him. "Thank you for saving my life. I've never been more scared of anything." I hugged him.

He hugged me back awkwardly. "You're welcome."

"Especially since they had guns." I blew out a breath.

"Guns?" Simon yelped, and I was hugging nothing but air.

I knelt and tapped his cheeks. "S-Man, come on. Wake up." I pulled a water bottle from my bag and splashed it on his face until he sat up, sputtering. "Ya with me?"

"Yeah." He flushed red. "Thanks for coming to my rescue. I guess we're even." He got to his feet. "What now?"

We heard a noise in the woods, and started running.

No words necessary!

16

TAKEN!

"Oh my God, Simon. I can't find my Digital Diva mask anywhere," I said into my cell hand that evening. The sun was starting to set, and I was trying not to freak out.

"What do you mean? You were wearing it when we ran out of the lab."

"I know, but it's gone now. I took it off after I left you. Maybe I dropped it."

"Did you check wherever you live? Where is that, by the way?"

"Thoroughly, and I'm still not telling you."

"Fine. It has to be somewhere in the woods between the university lab and your house."

"I retraced my steps. Twice! I still can't find it. You know how I told you Sam knows me? Well, I called her and she agreed to meet you in the woods to help look for it? If anyone finds that mask, my cover will be blown and my life will be ruined."

"Girls. You're all so dramatic."

"Please Simon. I could really use your help."

He hesitated, then finally sighed. "I'm on my way."

Fifteen minutes later, Simon showed up, and my mouth opened as wide as the crater that meteor had made.

"I can see your tonsils, you know."

"Sorry. You look amazing. What did you do?"

He reddened, but I could tell he was pleased. "Followed some advice Digital Diva gave me."

I scanned his slim fitting jeans, long sleeved white ribbed shirt with the tight graphic T-shirt over the top. "You put that outfit together all on your own?"

"I'm not stupid. I asked the store clerk to give me whatever was in style."

"You look fantastic," slipped out of my mouth.

"F-Fantastic?" he sputtered, his fair skin flushing a bright pink. "You really think so?"

I paused, then decided he more than anyone deserved a little confidence boost. "Yeah." I smiled, eyeing his thick russet colored curls that had been cut and styled perfectly, tawny eyes with lashes even longer than mine, and a sculpted mouth to die for that framed his blazing white teeth.

Maria was gonna love him.

"Cool." He shoved his hands into his pockets, beaming. "Now what?"

"We look one more time. This Digital Diva stuff is pretty weird, huh? Any idea who she is?"

He stared at me until I started to squirm, and then said, "No clue. You?"

Maybe telling him Digital Diva knew Sam wasn't such a good idea. "Nope," I answered firmly. I just met her through Mel, and since Mel's not home, she called me for help." Now that I said it out loud, it sounded weak.

"How come you're not out with Mel? I haven't seen you

around much this week. Everything okay?" He narrowed his eyes.

I shrugged. "Just not feeling myself lately. Nasty headaches."

"Probably from straining your brain." He nudged me and chuckled. "I heard about your photographic memory. All that information memorized in one brain is enough to give anyone headaches."

"Funny. We'd better get started before it gets too late. Lead the way, and we'll retrace the steps you and Digital Diva took."

After scouring the area with no luck, Simon said, "Maybe some animal took it back to its nest. We should probably go. It's getting dark. I heard on the weather channel there was a big storm headed our way. A possible tornado warning."

"Nah, there's not enough convection in the upper atmosphere. I doubt we'll get an actual tornado ... uh, but what do I know." I laughed, sounding like a sick hyena.

"Right." He quirked his brow at me, then glanced up at the darkening sky loaded with rain clouds. "It would stink getting stuck in that."

"No kidding." We started heading back with me leading the way. The wind picked up and temperature dropped a few degrees.

Simon shielded his face from the rain. "This is torture."

"Gotcha!" Mel appeared from out of nowhere.

Simon and I both jumped a foot. "Ohmigod, Mel, you scared me half to death. What are you doing here?"

"I'm on my way home. Remember the party at that new spot in the woods you refused to go to?"

"Oh, right."

"Everyone was asking about you."

"Everyone?"

"Okay, not everyone, but Maria wanted you to come as much as I did."

"Was Trevor there?"

"Yeah, and so was Ali. She's staking her claim, big-time. Trevor was actually talking to her and smiling. You should have been there."

"After the trouble we all got in last time, you're crazy."

"More like desperate. And bored. You don't want to do anything anymore."

"Sorry. I've been in enough trouble lately, and I'm sure no one wanted me to ruin this party, too. If Sheriff Hamilton had shown up, you'd all probably be grounded for like ever."

"Just promise me you'll show up for the Thanksgiving festival tomorrow. Ali's dad is having another fundraiser. It should be fun."

"I'm sure my parents will make me go anyway."

"I'll be there, too, Mel," Simon said from a few feet away.

Mel looked to the side and did a double-take. "Simon? I didn't even see you there. I mean, you look ... whoa!" She couldn't stop staring at him. "What are you doing here?"

"Helping Sam look for Digital Diva's mask," Simon said, standing a little straighter. "I know her, too, now. She lost it after the mission we went on together."

"Crazy dude say what?" Mel gaped at me.

"Yeah, can you believe it? It's a long story. I'm sure Simon would love to tell you all about it." I pleaded with her, giving her my best I-need-you-sidekick look. This was as close to a date as I could get for Simon. The rest was up to him. Not to mention it would take his mind off his doubts about me.

Mel looked from me to Simon to me again, and then shrugged. "I'm always up for a good story."

"Well, um, since I already heard the story, I'll catch up with you later. My mom will kill me if she finds out I'm gone."

Her look said you so owe me, but it didn't have half as much heat as it used to. She studied Simon carefully, then looped her arm through his. "All right, Simon, you can fill me in while you walk me home."

Simon was so stunned he forgot all about me and let Mel walk him off in one direction, while I cut through the woods the other way as quick as I could. I had almost made it home, when I ran into the queen of she-devils.

Alison Tucker.

"Well if it isn't Surfer Girl." She didn't even try to be nice since no one was around. "Aren't you afraid you're going to melt?" She crossed her arms over her sporty raincoat and matching boots. "You're too late for the party if that's where you're headed. It's been cancelled."

I tried to step around her, refusing to let her bait me.

She blocked my path. "No one wanted you there, anyway. This is my town," Ali said, poking me hard in the chest. "Trevor is mine, too."

I gasped. "I'm sure Trevor can make up his own mind."

"He was at the party with me. I'd say his mind is already made up. If you know what's good for you, you'll stay far away from him and all my friends. Why don't you do us all a favor and go back to LA where you belong?"

"Or else?"

"I'll continue to print rumors in the school paper and make your life miserable. We clear?"

I didn't say a word, just stepped around her and she let me this time. But I couldn't deny she was right about one thing. Trevor had obviously moved on.

And I had to let him, no matter how much it broke my heart.

THAT NIGHT I FRANTICALLY SEARCHED MY HOUSE AGAIN FOR my mask, but I couldn't find it anywhere. It hadn't been in the woods, either. If anyone found that, I was in so much trouble. My DNA was all over it.

"Looking for this, Digital Diva?"

I whirled around and gaped as Gram handed me my folded and pressed mask.

"Mom never does my laundry," was all I could think to say.

"We both know I'm not your mother," Gram responded dryly, set the laundry basket down, then took me in her arms and hugged me tight. "I'm here for you, Sammy, same as I've always been."

I closed my eyes and hugged her back ... then cried my eyes out like a baby.

After what felt like forever, Gram said, "Feel better?"

I stepped back, nodded hard, and blew my nose. "Much. I've been so scared, and the only one who knows is Mel. Gram, you have no idea what's going on. It's all so messed up. I don't want any of this, but I can't make it go away."

She sat down on my bed, pulled me with her, and smoothed back my hair. "Then maybe it's time you told me everything."

I started from the beginning and filled her in on every last detail, the story pouring out of me. Gram looked a bit shocked and a whole lot worried, but she never once freaked out. I should have known I could trust her, and it felt good not to be alone. I had Mel, but she was a sidekick.

Gram was my mentor, my rock.

"The government might not have done anything illegal," Gram said, "but I can see why your father didn't like some of the things they were doing, much less being involved in them."

"Is that what Mom and Dad fought about last year?"

"What your father was involved in was classified. He couldn't tell her the details, but she knew he was upset. Only she pushed him not to make waves. They are too different kinds of people, Sammy. Neither one bad, just different. Some people aren't meant to be together."

I cried again, and she hugged me close once more. "Do you think Dad will at least stay in Blue Lake? I don't like him living so far away."

"Anything is possible." Gram wiped my eyes, but I could tell even she doubted that would ever happen. "Get to bed, and don't worry. I'll figure something out. We'll talk in the morning, okay?"

"Okay." I smiled, crawling into bed exhausted. "Thanks Gram. I couldn't do this without you."

"Good. Because you ever try to again, I'll paddle your behind myself." She winked.

I slept sound for the first time since this whole thing started.

THE NEXT MORNING I HEARD THE WINDOW BEING CLOSED IN my bedroom. I smiled, yawning and stretching as I rolled over to say good morning to Gram, then bolted upright.

Scary Tall Guy and Scary Short Guy had opened my window and climbed inside. I tried to scream, but the short guy slapped a cloth over my nose and mouth, and I passed out within seconds.

Sometime later I blinked my eyes to a bright light, my wrists and ankles chafing against the tight rope tied around them. Still in my pajamas, I sat up, scooting back against the rock wall behind me. We were in some kind of cave, but that didn't help much. This was the Adirondacks. There were caves everywhere!

"Hey, the kid's awake." Scary Tall Guy stopped playing solitaire and tapped Scary Short Guy's shoulder.

"Too bad she wasn't that Digital Diva kid. I still owe the brat," the short guy grumbled.

"Never mind her. It's this kid we want."

They didn't know I was Digital Diva, yet they'd kidnapped me anyway. What could they possibly want with Sam? "If you want money, I'm sure my parents will pay."

They looked at each other and laughed, then Scary Tall Guy said, "Money is of no concern to us."

"T-Then what do you want from me?" I asked, terrified of what their answer might be.

"Shut up, kid. It's not you we want anything from. You'd better pray Mommy and Daddy come through." Scary Short Guy grabbed his cell phone and tossed it to his partner.

The tall man dialed a number then held the phone out in front of my face. "Speak."

"No." I stuck out my chin, feeling brave.

His short partner slapped me across the face, smiling evilly. "Do it."

"Ow." I licked my lip, tasting the metallic flavor of blood, and then my bravery evaporated as I realized I was dressed as Sam. Not Digital Diva. "I don't know what to say," I said in a small voice. "You didn't have to hit me."

"That's enough. The girl's time will come. For now, we

need her alive," the tall guy said to his partner, then held the phone to his ear. "You heard her voice, now give us the information we want in one hour or she's dead. And no cops." He hung up.

She's dead echoed in my ears over and over. I felt helpless just sitting there all tied up. But then it hit me. I wasn't helpless. I'd survived an amazing encounter with a meteor for God's sake. I'd saved Old Lady Lipowitz, Frat Boy, and Blonde Barbie. And I'd outwitted these thugs a couple times. No, I wasn't helpless at all because I had a secret weapon of my own. Digital Diva. I was a superhero.

Maybe it was time I started acting like one.

17

THE PARTY'S OVER ... OR NOT

My abductors played a card game of poker and made bets while they waited for my parents to call back. They really didn't see me as a threat; they only saw me as Sam. Well, Sam wasn't a wimp, either. Sam was Digital Diva. I could do this. I just needed to think.

The phone rang, and I flinched. I needed more time.

The tall man walked to the corner of the cave, out of earshot, and got in a heated discussion with whoever was on the other end of the line. I needed to hear that conversation. Thinking quickly, I made a fist, then flung my hand open, shooting an electric pulse from my cell palm until it tapped into the phone conversation wirelessly. Voices echoed in my ears, in between bits of static.

"You fools better not screw up again," said the smooth cultured voice on the other end of the phone. "This ends now! Everything I've worked for is riding on this deal. I need that Electro Wave."

I stifled a gasp. Congressman Tucker? Ali had the nerve to say _my_ father had done something illegal. Focusing, I twitched my cheek to turn on the video camera in my head, then wiggled my nose to record video of these men. Pulling on my ear, the audio clicked on and started recording the phone conversation.

"But, Boss, it's not our fault the other leads turned up nothing. We're working as hard and as fast as we can," the tall man said coolly.

"You want your cut of the money, you will work harder and do as I say," the congressman continued. "I want those blueprints by the end of the festival. If I have to intervene, your payoff goes down." He ended the call.

The tall guy shot a glance in my direction, then walked over to the short guy as they both started speaking in Arabic. I kept the camera rolling and clicked my tongue to switch on the Rosetta Stone Deluxe translator my Electro Wave came equipped with.

"He thinks he's so tough. He would be nothing without us. People are tired of war. Keeping our people in business, keeps his pro military platform in the spotlight," Scary Tall Guy grumbled. "Yet we get no thanks. We've done all the work. It might have been his idea to kidnap her," he jerked his head in my direction, "but we were the ones to pull off the job."

I froze, acting like I was in a daze, praying they wouldn't figure out what I was up to. Congressman Tucker was funding terrorists? What about his "We don't negotiate with terrorists" motto on all his campaign posters? A whole lot more than just his smile was phony.

"What's wrong with her eyes," Scary Short Guy said. "They're open real wide like she's not right in the head. It gives me the creeps."

"Nah," Scary Tall Guy said. "She's probably just in shock. Doesn't matter much anyways. She's not gonna live after we get those blueprints."

I tried not to gasp and pretended to itch my ears, pulling on my lobes to turn up the volume on my internal microphone. My eyes were burning from not blinking, but I needed to stay focused on the men so the video camera wouldn't miss a thing. Not right in the head? If they only knew. A bubble of hysteria gurgled in my throat and I giggled.

"I don't care what you say, that girl's mental." Scary Short Guy slapped down a card. "I'll bet her parents come through with the blueprints for the Electro Wave with ten minutes to spare."

"I'll see your bet and raise you. Boss is a master manipulator. He'll make sure of it."

"No kidding. He's so power hungry, he'd do anything to gain a faster trip to the White House. Stupid, naïve people. All his so-called trips to the Middle East as a peace negotiator were really back room deals to keep people like us in power by sharing top secret information."

Bingo. I had all the proof I needed. I saved the video tape and filed it in my brain. Now I just had to escape and stop my parents from giving these creeps the blueprints.

Pushing my fear aside, I moved my hands around on the floor of the cave slowly, so they wouldn't notice, then my fingers touched a sharp rock. This could work. I tried to cut the rope but my fingers cramped. It was no use. I felt the knot, and the Girl Scout in me squealed silently with delight. This was no knot. This was a joke.

No match for Troup Leader Sam.

Within minutes I had the knot undone, but I sat still, forming a game plan. Even with my Digital Diva abilities, I couldn't take these thugs. This cave didn't have much I could use to defeat them with my brains, either. I scanned the dwelling, and did a double take, staring up with a grin.

But it did have something else that just might be perfect.

"Hey, she doesn't look in shock anymore," Scary Short Guy stood. "Why's she looking up at the ceiling?"

Scary Tall Guy stood. "Get her."

I scrambled to my feet, stumbling back and trying not to trip over my nightgown. Think, Sam ... Sonar! That's it. I turned around and faced the men, who stopped short for a second. A second was all I needed. I held my breath, and pushed all the blood to my face as hard as I could.

An ultra-sonic sound pulsed out my earsin waves, sending a message to the sleeping bats above.

Danger!

The bats shrieked and flapped their wings, descending in a flurry. Batting the air, they swarmed all around the cave looking for a way out. I dove to the ground while the men swatted at the air, stumbling about and covering their heads. I crawled out the opening of the cave as fast as I could.

I had a madman to stop.

PUSHING THE GAS PEDAL OF THE BAD GUYS' DARK SEDAN TO the floor, I picked up speed and raced to the center of town where the festival was being held. I'd found the car parked just outside of the cave, and hotwired it, using my mental GPS to direct me to the festival. The parade was over, and all the citizens were gathered in the town square for Congressman Tucker's fundraiser festival and speech.

I hit the brakes and the tires squealed, kicking up fall leaves and dirt as I spun the car 180 degrees and parked a perfect 6 inches from the curb.

Sheriff Hamilton raced in after me, sirens wailing and lights flashing. He flew from his car, drew his gun, and yelled, "This is the police. Put your hands in the air and slowly step out of the car."

They couldn't see inside the tinted windows. For all they knew, the bad guys were inside. Carefully opening the door, I climbed out, hands up high.

Everyone gasped.

Ali said, "I knew she was up to no good. Can't we have her arrested, Daddy?"

"Be quiet, Alison," the congressman said sternly, a worried look crossing his face.

"Underage driving again, Miss Granger?" Sheriff Hamilton raised a brow as he lowered his gun. "And why are you in your pajamas?" Obviously my parents hadn't gone to the police, just like the thugs had ordered, but where were they?

"Oh, thank God you're safe, Sammy," Gram ran over to me and tried to pull me in a hug.

"No," I shouted, and Gram blinked.

"What's going on, Sam?" Trevor stepped forward, away from Ali.

"Yeah, Sam, what happened?" Mel joined him.

"Just a sec. I need to talk to my grandmother, then I'll explain about the car and why I'm dressed this way. I promise," I said to the sheriff, and he nodded his consent. The crowd's murmur increased as I pulled Gram off to the side. "Where are Mom and Dad?" I asked again, more urgently this time.

She leaned in close and whispered for my ears only, "At Electro to look for the 'you know what.' Your parents were told not to go to the police, so they went to Congressman Tucker instead since he's familiar with terrorists groups and how they operate. Even though he said it was against his better judgment, he advised them to turn over the information for your sake."

"I'll bet he did. Gram, call them and tell them I'm safe and not to give any information to anyone. Not even people they think they can trust, okay?" She nodded and pulled out her phone as I turned to Dark Shades Man. "Agent Maxwell?"

He nodded slowly, not really looking surprised.

"You might want to watch this video. Do you mind if I use your laptop, Congressman Tucker?"

"Well, I don't know. I--" He started backing away.

"Thanks!" I plugged a memory stick into the laptop the congressman was using to project his plan for lowering the crime rate in Blue Lake if re-elected. The video I'd filmed of the terrorists flashed across the huge screen and the audio I'd recorded of the congressman's phone conversation poured out the speakers.

The congressman's face paled and he turned to flee. Sheriff Hamilton started to chase him. Making a detour, the Congressman pulled out a gun and locked his arm around Trevor's neck.

"Daddy," Ali sobbed. "What's happening?"

I sucked in a breath, my heart racing and palms sweating as I locked eyes on Trevor.

The congressman kept quiet, staring down Trevor's dad. "Drop the gun, sheriff."

Sheriff Hamilton froze, cursed, then lowered his gun, looking helpless and frustrated. "You hurt my boy, Tucker, I'll kill you myself."

I had to do something. Suddenly I remembered intense excitement made me block calls, whereas intense fear made me set off alarms. I channeled all the fear I felt for Trevor, letting it flood my every pore.

Every car alarm within a mile started blaring, including the wail of police cars, fire engines, and ambulances. The noise was so loud and unexpected, people covered their ears and dropped to the ground out of instinct.

Including Congressman Tucker.

I flew into action, racing over and karate chopping the gun out of the Congressman's hand. Stumbling back, I tried to catch my breath, exhausted from the use of my Electro Wave. I'd pushed myself to the limit this time, and I wasn't sure I could recover. I struggled not to black out, knowing I had to hold it together until this was over.

It took Sheriff Hamilton only seconds to tackle the Congressman and slap the cuffs on him, then wrap his son in his arms for a bear hug. No one said a word as Ali's mom led her away, tears streaming down her face. The Burdick twins followed quietly at a distance behind her. Everyone else gathered around to try to figure out how all the alarms in town had gone off at the same time. Better yet, how to shut them off.

I gave Agent Maxwell the location of the cave.

"You okay? You don't look so good," he said.

"Been through a lot. Probably in shock or something," I said, which was true.

He studied me. "Tell me one thing. How'd you escape?"

"Digital Diva."

His eyes flashed and then he slipped his glasses on, but didn't say a word.

"She showed up and tapped into the bad guys' phone and recorded them," I quickly added. "It was crazy. I was so scared, but she was awesome. She did this sonic boom thing that sent bats flying everywhere like something right out of a horror movie. It freaked me out, but she pushed me out the door, hotwired the car and told me to drive myself here and give you the recording. Said it was time for her to go, whatever that meant. I'm just glad she was there when I needed her."

"I'll bet you were." Agent Maxwell got in his car and drove off.

My world turned black.

"Sam? Aw, God, Sam, please be okay." A familiar male voice said from somewhere close to my face.

I felt a tap on my forehead, then someone brushed my hair aside and took my face in their big hands. Warm breath caressed my cheeks seconds before a pair of firm lips pressed against mine. Stars shined bright behind my eyes, fireworks exploded in my mind, and tingles raced up and down my spine.

I must be dreaming, or dead, but I didn't care. I didn't want to wake up because I was in heaven. The lips lingered a moment longer, then finally pulled away. I struggled to open my eyes only to stare up into the most glorious sight of all. Trevor's face.

Trevor Hamilton had finally kissed me.

Thank God I'd been half out of it since I still had no control over what he did to my body. This was not the time to get sent to the rescue.

"Move out of the way, boy. What's the matter with you? Can't you see the girl needs some air?" Gram snapped.

Trevor smiled slow and sweet. "Glad to have you back, Samo."

"Glad to be back, Trevo." I matched his smile, letting my eyes say what I knew my mouth never could.

Gram budged in between us. "You scared me half to death, child." She pulled me to my feet and hugged me hard. I hugged her back harder. "We need to call your parents."

"Do you have a phone?" I asked her.

"Do you need one?" She raised a brow at me.

I looked beyond her and saw a group of my friends waiting to talk to me. Sam, not Digital Diva, just Sam. Simon and Maria stood together, holding hands. Guess he and Mel had decided they were better off friends, and he'd opened his eyes to someone who liked him for who he was. And Scott had finally smartened up and asked Mel to be his girlfriend. Big Matt stood by them ... and even Trevor stood front and center. Leave it to Mel to straighten everything out for me in true sidekick form.

"Can you make the call, Gram?" I asked.

Her gaze followed mine to the grinning faces staring at me in awe. Complete and utter acceptance. Like I was one of them.

She winked. "You go ahead, honey. I'd say you've done enough, my little hero."

———

"I STILL CAN'T BELIEVE EVERYTHING THAT WENT DOWN, AND now nothing. No tourists, no scientists, no bad guys, no government agents. It's weird," Mel said as she sat beside me on my dad's couch.

"Weird but awesome. Trust me, no more Digital Diva is something to give thanks for." I plopped my slippered feet on the coffee table in front of us. "I've had all the excitement I can take for one school year."

"How are your headaches?"

"Much better. I can handle being a brainiac, it's the rescue missions my body can't take. But I haven't had an episode in so long I even convinced my parents to cancel the neurological tests I was scheduled for."

"I'm glad you're finally getting back to yourself, and I told you Trevor liked you. He kissed you."

"He thought I was dying. He gave me mouth-to-mouth. It didn't mean anything. You know we can only be friends." I acted nonchalant, afraid to read anything more into it than that. Afraid to hope we could have more. I'd come to accept if I wanted to keep Digital Diva in retirement, then dating was out of the question. But my heart knew that had been a real kiss, no matter what my head said.

"You'll find a way to be with him, I'm sure of it. Just give it time. At least you got your first kiss, that's a start." Mel hugged me. "Can you believe Ali's dad was involved? She's not so high and mighty now."

"I feel sorry for her. I know what it's like to have your dad sent away. Thank God they caught those terrorists."

"Any word on your parents?"

"Well, they're not together if that's what you mean, but at least they're talking. Dad leaves at the end of the month, and guess what. Simon is going to intern for him back in San Jose over the winter break. Isn't that wild?" Mel just rolled her eyes, but even she had to admit Simon had turned out to be pretty cool. "At least Gram's staying on."

"Good. You need a mentor because being your sidekick was getting exhausting."

"Who are you kidding? You loved every minute of it, but hopefully there won't be a need for Digital Diva again anytime soon."

"What now?"

"I keep looking for a way out of this mess while keeping myself out of the spotlight," I said. "I just want to go back to school and get back to normal ... whatever that is."

"I have to say normal was pretty boring before the diva

came along. At least things got exciting in Blue Lake for a while."

"We'll just have to make our own excitement, now that everyone has accepted me."

"You're right. We don't need Digital Diva to have fun. We just need each other." We high fived.

This really was turning out to be the best year ever. Trevor gave me my first kiss, I'd made some really great friends, and my parents were spending a lot more time with me. All in all, being hard wired wasn't so bad. I wasn't afraid anymore.

I was fearless.

The doorbell rang, so we both went to answer it. No one was there, just a package on the front steps. I opened it and gasped. A brand new Digital Diva costume, only this one was fantastic. A shimmery silver spandex unitard with a bejeweled turquoise belt, matching boots and mask. And the words Digital Diva were embroidered across the front.

"What does it mean," Mel asked.

"I don't know," I answered, looking up just in time to see Dark Shades Man climb into his car and drive away.

Agent Maxwell.

Seconds later my hand vibrated, and I jumped. I pulled off my glove and saw that I had a text message, only it was from an undisclosed number. I clicked on it and gulped.

"What's wrong," Mel asked, leaning over to see my hand.

I looked at her in shock. So much for being fearless. I was scared to death. "It's a message." I could barely speak, but the message written on my palm would be forever burned into my brain. I held my hand out to her. "See."

. . .

WE KNOW WHO YOU ARE, SAMANTHA GRANGER. THE ELECTRO Wave has

a tracking number embedded on the inside. It was only a

matter of time before we found you. We'll be in touch, and

we'll be watching. Remember, the Government has ways of

making anything disappear. Including you, Digital Diva.

THEY COULDN'T FORCE ME TO BE DIGITAL DIVA ... COULD they?

ABOUT THE AUTHOR

Kari Lee Townsend is a National Bestselling Author of mysteries & a tween superhero series. She also writes romance and women's fiction as Kari Lee Harmon. With a background in English education, she's now a full-time writer, wife to her own superhero, mom of 3 sons, 1 darling diva, 1 daughter-in-law & 2 lovable fur babies. These days you'll find her walking her dogs or hard at work on her next story, living a blessed life.

ALSO BY THE AUTHOR

Sleeping in the Middle

MERRY SCROOGE-MAS SERIES

Naughty or Nice

Sleigh Bells Ring

Jingle All The Way

LAKE HOUSE TREASURES SERIES

The Beginning

Amber

Meghan

Brook